"Don't touch me! Isn't Julie enough for you?"

Romy's voice was quavering as she tried to deflect his advances. Quila emitted a soft, slightly deprecating laugh. "Julie is a beautiful woman, but she doesn't kiss the way you do."

"That's too bad, isn't it?" In spite of her bravado and her response delivered in a hard, sarcastic tone, Romy had to acknowledge that he was unnerving her in a manner she had never known before, and her stomach muscles started to knot.

"But most importantly," he continued, "I don't see the promise in her eyes that I see in yours."

"What on earth are you talking about...?" she stammered, backing away.

"You know only too well what I'm talking about," Quila said, reaching for her.... And there was no evading him or obstructing his purpose.

WELCOME
TO THE WONDERFUL WORLD
OF *Harlequin Romances*

Interesting, informative and entertaining, each Harlequin Romance portrays an appealing and original love story. With a varied array of settings, we may lure you on an African safari, to a quaint Welsh village, or an exotic Riviera location—anywhere and everywhere that adventurous men and women fall in love.

As publishers of Harlequin Romances, we're extremely proud of our books. Since 1949, Harlequin Enterprises has built its publishing reputation on the solid base of quality and originality. Our stories are the most popular paperback romances sold in North America; every month, six new titles are released and sold at nearly every book-selling store in Canada and the United States.

A free catalog listing all Harlequin Romances can be yours by writing to the

HARLEQUIN READER SERVICE,
(In the U.S.) 1440 South Priest Drive, Tempe, AZ 85281
(In Canada) Stratford, Ontario, N5A 6W2

We sincerely hope you enjoy reading this Harlequin Romance.

Yours truly,

THE PUBLISHERS
Harlequin Romances

Summerhaze

Kate O'Hara

Harlequin Books

TORONTO • NEW YORK • LOS ANGELES • LONDON
AMSTERDAM • PARIS • SYDNEY • HAMBURG
STOCKHOLM • ATHENS • TOKYO • MILAN

Original hardcover edition published in 1982
by Mills & Boon Limited

ISBN 0-373-02560-2

Harlequin Romance first edition July 1983

CHAPTER ONE

ROMY Palliser pulled up at the kerb opposite number 28 Watson Avenue and with customary deftness switched off the ignition, removed the keys and her sunglasses and reached for her holdall which lay on the back seat. She paused for a cursory inspection of her reflection in the rear vision mirror before climbing from the rental car and then, still playing for time, slowly stretched her cramped limbs and swung the car door closed. Finally it was locked and there was nothing left for her to do but to lift her head and take stock of her surroundings. She did so reluctantly, waiting for the upsurge of panic, dread, the clamour of an inner voice crying, 'What *have* I done?' But like the times before, it never came.

The street hadn't changed. In five years it hadn't changed! Just as Masterton itself seemed not to have changed. Why was it so hard to believe? And why was it so easy to feel that the past five years had been nothing more than a brief flight of fancy? It all might never have been. She might never have left this place. And she grieved for the five years even while she gazed about her and experienced a peace she had never expected to find at being home once more.

The mid-morning sun shone down on the quiet street lined either side with elm-studded grass verges. Quaint old colonial cottages stood back from front gardens bright with spring flowers and blossoming trees which overhung wooden picket or bush fences and contrasted delicately with a vibrant blue sky.

'I'd forgotten how blue the sky could be,' Romy mused, and at that moment her attention was caught by the opening of the front door of number 28. Her heart leapt in much the same way as it had when the aircraft had broken through the grey mantle of cloud and she had set eyes on the rich green hill country of her native land for the first time in five years.

Her face brightened and her eyes lit up. It was Nellie—and someone else. She narrowed her gaze, an action that availed her nothing, for still the man remained unrecognisable. But Nellie ... Romy switched her attention once more—even she hadn't appeared to have changed. Her hair was a trifle whiter perhaps, but her little figure was as erect as ever. Buoyed up with a sense of urgency and anticipation, Romy swung the strap of her holdall over her shoulder and swiftly crossed the road. She couldn't wait to see her face.

The man was straightening after giving Nellie a farewell kiss and by the time Romy had reached the gate he was half way down the narrow rose-bordered path. She unlatched the gate and pushed it wide, deciding to wait until the man had passed through before entering. Beyond him she saw Nellie standing on the verandah in an attitude of waiting, her hands resting down flat on her aproned thighs and her body inclining to one side to see around the figure of the man. There was no recognition evident on her face, just a query, then came a slight frown. Romy grinned, more to herself than at Nellie, and gave her a wave and was thrilled to see the woman's diminutive figure give a jig of recognition and excitement.

By this time the man had reached the gate and Romy saved the dying embers of her smile for him. ''Morning,' she said, and as her eyes came to encounter his she felt a swift and astounding change take place within her. It was as though her body had been pierced through suddenly and filled with a strange heat, sharp and pleasurable, which in turn caused the surface of her skin to become more moist than it was already. Her smile died and was gone in a flash and she wasn't even aware of it. The only response the man gave to her greeting was the briefest of nods. His dark brown eyes continued to bore into hers for a second or two longer before he passed through the gate and strode across the road to where a blue automatic car was parked a short distance in front of hers. As she turned to stare after his retreating figure, she did so in wonder.

It wasn't the first time she had experienced such a chemical reaction—which was the only definition she was ever able to come up and attach to the experience— but neither, on the other hand, did they occur frequently, nor were they sparked off by men similar in colouring or appearance. One factor they all had in common, however, was that such sparks invariably dwindled with subsequent encounters with the men concerned, and even despite this foreknowledge, Romy had never failed yet to be shaken by them and made curious by the men who could trigger them.

'Sunshine! Is that you? Is that really you, or are my eyes playing me false?'

Romy turned back to the little elderly woman teetering with impatience on the verge of the verandah steps, and was swamped with a feeling of gladness that thrust all thought of the man from her mind. 'Of course they're not playing you false, Nellie,' she admonished, starting up the path. 'You've always had the keenest eyesight of anyone I've ever known.' And with a laugh, she dropped her holdall on to the verandah, enfolded

Nellie in her arms and treated her to a warm abandoned hug.

'Sunshine! Well, my goodness, what a surprise! Let me look at you. I see it, but I can't believe it yet. Now stand back and let me look at you.'

Obediently, Romy stood back, and in spite of her smile, the moisture in Nellie's eyes caused tears to prick sharply in her own.

'You've changed,' said Nellie bluntly, and her tone wasn't one of approval.

'Well, you haven't,' Romy responded with a laugh and another hug. 'Five years, and you're still as sprightly as ever.'

'Nonsense!' Nellie refuted. 'I'm getting on and can't do as much as I used to. I'm seventy now, you know. Come in, come in—or are you wanting to be off?' She turned back to look at her. 'The young are always wanting to rush off these days—never in one place for five minutes.'

Romy laughed. 'No, I wanted to see you before I go on out to Summerhaze. I also want to talk to you about Pop. And change too, if I may. I feel as though I've been in these clothes for a week!' And she followed after her along the spacious hall, with its walls a-clutter with pictures, and into the sunny homely kitchen Romy had always loved from when she was a child.

'Sunshine, they all called you when you were younger,' said Nellie, pouring hot water from the kettle into an old china teapot which was as familiar to Romy as was Nellie herself. She pulled on a knitted tea-cosy and carried the pot across to the collapsible breakfast table affixed to the wall. 'Not much sunshine about you now,' she went on with the characteristic forthrightness of the very young and the old.

'Oh? Why? I didn't think I'd changed that much.'

Romy's eyes twinkled at her mischievously, and she helped herself to a scone smeared liberally with home-made jam.

'You're far too skinny. You look emaciated.'

'I'm a model, Nellie, and models have to be slim.'

'Slim, my eye! You're positively gaunt, pallid, and you've got a twang—and you've done something to your beautiful hair.' Her alert brown eyes, registering disgust, skimmed over Romy's long hair, a darker blonde than she could remember it having been. 'And you've straightened it, too.'

'It's not dyed, Nellie,' Romy told her, disguising her laughter. 'Nor has it been straightened. It's gone darker from being so long in the northern hemisphere, I expect, and it seems to have straightened out a little— why, I don't know. Maybe it's the water over there— or the pollution. But don't worry, Nellie, after a summer back here it will be back to what it was, and so will I.'

'A summer, you say? You'll be off before the end of the summer, that's what I think.' Nellie began pouring the tea. 'Like Quila.'

'Quila?'

'My nephew. You bumped into him at the gate. When he returned from America he couldn't settle. He'd have been off again if he hadn't been tied here with a number of commitments.'

'Was he your nephew? I never knew you had a nephew, Nellie.'

'A great nephew, actually. And a bit of a rebel. He left New Zealand for far-flung horizons when he was just eighteen—like you. And like you, I can't see him settling down here.'

'Well, of course, I can't speak for him, but I think perhaps I've had enough,' said Romy. 'Five years of the kind of life and success I've had has made me think only of myself. I should have come home before this, for a holiday at least. I could have done so easily, but instead I spent the time and money flitting off to France or down to the Caribbean.'

'You're only young once. It's natural to want to make the most of it. If the young weren't selfish to a certain extent many things in this world would never get done,' observed Nellie.

'But not at the expense of one's family. I realise now that I've put myself first all along.' Romy sighed and looked across at Nellie anxiously. 'How is Pop, Nellie? How is he really? How long has he been ill, and why wasn't I told?'

'If you weren't told, how do you know he's ill?'

'I was on holiday in London. My contract in New York was at an end and I was considering an offer to move away from New York to London. I had been there only a matter of days when I bumped into Mr and Mrs Reilly—do you know the Reillys? They own a farm farther north of ours.'

'Yes, I think so. I went to school with Mark Reilly's older sister, if I remember rightly,' said Nellie.

'I couldn't believe my eyes when I saw them window shopping in Piccadilly. We had lunch together and they spoke to me of Pop's illness as though I knew all about it, which I didn't. I can't understand why Mum didn't write to me—or Julie. I would have thought my own sister would have felt that I had a right to know.'

'I suspect they wanted to keep it from you. Judging from your letters, you were happy and doing so well over there, and they didn't want to spoil it for you . . .'

'But it was a massive coronary, wasn't it? Two years ago?'

After a small hesitation, Nellie nodded. 'Yes,' she

admitted. 'And it was touch and go for a while. But when your father first spoke it was to insist that you weren't to be worried. Your mother had tried before that to contact you, as soon as it had happened, but it seemed that you were away, because they simply couldn't reach you.'

'Oh!' Romy's exclamation was fraught with frustration. 'They should have kept trying. I had every right to be worried!' Abruptly, she bowed her head and sighed deeply, plucking at the cotton tablecloth, its fading embroidered pattern blurring still further as tears sprang to her eyes. She swallowed painfully. 'Oh, Nellie, I wish I'd known! I could have come home so easily.'

'And broken your contract?'

'No, but I could have made it home for a month at least.'

'And what good would that have done? You'd have been upset and forced to return to New York and exist in a state of perpetual anxiety.'

Romy's misted eyes lifted. 'You think it was the right thing to do, then? Not to tell me?'

'Sunshine,' Nellie leaned forward and covered Romy's hand with one of hers and gazed into her eyes, a rather sad expression reflected in her own, 'I don't know. One only really ever knows in retrospect what should have been said or exactly when it should have been said, if it should have in fact ever been said at all. I must keep my own counsel where you're concerned, whether I think it's right or not. Because I'm only a family friend, not family, so it's not my place to say things to you that I think should have been said some time ago.'

Romy frowned. 'You are talking about Pop, aren't you?' she asked, vaguely mystified.

Nellie gave a small sigh and patted her hand before withdrawing her own. 'Yes,' she said, somewhat wearily, Romy thought. 'We're talking about your father.'

'How is he, Nellie? Please tell me the truth.'

'He's slowed down a great deal. In that way you won't recognise him.'

'You mean he's grown old before his time?'

'Yes, I suppose that would sum it up,' Nellie agreed.

'How is he managing the farm, then?' Romy's voice rose with concern.

'That's something he'll discuss with you when you get home. He's looking very well considering, and the fact that he's been liberated from the worry he had initially has contributed to his present peace of mind. You'll see for yourself that all's going splendidly. Now tell me what you've been up to. Why aren't you married?'

Romy's wide smile appeared reluctantly, dispelling the anxiety in her expression. 'Oh, Nellie, I've had no time to establish any kind of friendship with a man, let alone contemplate marriage!'

'What?' exclaimed Nellie, giving the impression that she was appalled. 'No man?'

'Oh, plenty of men,' said Romy, twinkling audaciously, her bubbly humour returning. 'Why settle for one?'

'You're too fussy, that's your trouble. You'll end up on the shelf if you're not careful, my girl.'

'Really, Nellie! I'm only twenty-four. You'd have had me shackled at eighteen if you'd had your way!'

'It wouldn't have been such a bad thing. You'd have a couple of wee ones by this time and looking a whole lot healthier than you do now. What's all this travel succeeded in doing for you? Spoilt you, robbed you of the contentment of simply being here in this beautiful country where God put you and intended you to be. What good has it done you?'

Romy rose slowly to her feet and crossed over to the bench. Outside the sun was slanting through the spreading branches of the plum tree, not yet in blossom, and spilling through the window across the wood topped bench, scrubbed white by Nellie. 'You know, Nellie,' she said softly, 'I actually think I will want to stay.' She turned around to smile at the older woman. 'I admit I wasn't very sure at first. When I heard that Pop was ill, I didn't stop to think. I returned to New York and within two weeks I had my flight booked, relinquished the lease on my apartment and stored my belongings. The first opportunity I had to actually meditate on what all that meant was on the plane. Right up until that moment, Pop had been my major concern. Then, when I stopped over for a day in Honolulu and stood there in the sun, breathing in the sultry humid air and watching the rain falling only a matter of miles away, I suddenly thought: "This could be Auckland. I could be in Auckland!"' With a chuckle, Romy returned to her chair. She pushed her cup forward for the second cup of tea Nellie was offering and went on: 'I can laugh about it now, but I tell you, Nellie, I was panic-stricken! For the first time I realised what I was doing. I was going home. After five years of living and working in New York and travelling to all the capitals in the world, I was going home to a sixteen-hundred-acre farm somewhere at the back of beyond, and I was bathed in sweat that had nothing to do with the humidity of Honolulu, I can assure you.'

'But you didn't change your mind?'

'Oh, a hundred times. I've never felt so wretched or

so sick in all my life, as I did on that last leg. Then when I caught my first glimpse of land, my heart gave a tremendous leap. You know, I'd forgotten how green it was, how blue the sky is, how clean the air smells.'

'You'd forgotten a lot, then,' Nellie responded dryly.

'Oh, not really. Don't be so hard on me, Nellie,' Romy teased. 'There were times when I'd have given my right arm for some fresh farm milk straight from the cow, or vegetables straight out of the garden, and to eat fruit still warm from the east coast sun.'

'Well,' said Nellie with a full and relenting smile, 'it certainly did my old heart good to see you back, and it'll do Summerhaze no harm to have you back in residence for a time—no matter how short. Your mum and dad will be so thrilled to see you. I take it they don't know you're coming?'

Romy shook her head. 'I wanted to surprise them.'

'You'll certainly do that.' Nellie sighed. 'It'll be a powerful medicine for your father to have some sunshine about the place again.'

Romy laughed. 'So you don't think I've changed that drastically, then? I've not come back all cynical and world-weary?'

'Not you, Romy,' with a shake of her head. 'Never you.'

'I'm glad you have such faith in me,' Romy sparkled, and came around to give the older woman's shoulders another warm hug. 'And I'm also glad to see you looking so well.'

'Oh,' Nellie brushed this sentiment aside with a display of her customary brusqueness, 'never had a sick day in my life. Now go through to the bathroom and freshen up while I clear away here.'

Romy was exhausted really. The flight had been long

and the stopovers had seemed even longer, and although she had enjoyed the sixty-mile drive from Wellington, through the Rimutaka mountain range, to Masterton, she now felt almost at the end of her tether.

Perhaps a shower would revive her, she thought, as she slowly stripped off the clothes she had changed into during her stopover in Honolulu. The soap and water gliding over her skin was a luxury she would like to have prolonged, but she thought of a bed waiting for her at Summerhaze and hastened her movements. She had still a twenty-mile drive ahead of her.

She dressed quickly and yet with the care that her years as both a fashion and photographic model had instilled into her. It was important to her that she appear as attractive as she could, as much for her parents' benefit as for her own.

Arriving from a New York autumn and entering into a southern hemisphere spring, Romy found the climate temperate enough to don the silky yellow summer dress and matching short-sleeved, button-free jacket she had purchased on the spur of the moment in Honolulu. The dress was a simple yet flattering creation, gathered around the waist, its bodice supported by narrow shoulder straps.

Having fastened the stiff fabric belt about her waist, she reached for the fine gold chain, clasped it around her neck and readorned her fingers and wrists with the rings and bracelets she had set down on the vanity unit. Swiftly, but skilfully, she made up her face, finishing with a touch of dusky rose lipstick that corresponded perfectly with her long painted and manicured nails. As she touched a few drops of l'Air du Temps cologne to her neck and wrists, she caught her own tired, dispassionate gaze in the oval mirror that overhung the washbasin.

'Beautiful,' they described her. But she knew she certainly wasn't beautiful and she had no desire to be so. Her looks were 'in,' that was all. The line of her unplucked eyebrows was part of her charm, it was said, lending a hint of roguishness to eyes which were of no definite shape but which, by way of redemption, narrowed enchantingly when she smiled or laughed, their pale clear olive green owning a tendency to glint silver in certain lights. Her nose was somewhat out of character, for being straight, fine, with a rather aristocratic tilt at its very tip, it was at stark variance with her untamed hair, laughter-filled eyes, not to mention her famous gamine smile which revealed that her front two teeth were set back a fraction from the rest. By no means were they perfect, her New York agent had had to admit, but he justified what could possibly be viewed as a flaw by insisting that they were 'engagingly different'.

Yes, she thought to herself as she carried out her impartial examination, the only explanation she could offer for her success was that she had happened to be an entrant for the Miss Universe contest at the right time, when, at eighteen, her type of features were in vogue. The fact that she hadn't won the competition hadn't bothered her too greatly. She had had a very enjoyable and interesting time. And when the judges had awarded her the Miss Photogenic title, she was sure she couldn't have been more delighted. She had never had any illusions of grandeur about herself and hadn't began to entertain any even then. The only reason she had entered the competition in New Zealand to qualify as a New Zealand contestant was because several friends had dared her to. As far as anything else was concerned, she had always considered that she had her priorities right, that home and her family were her greatest loves, and she had never, not once, given a single thought to the opportunities such an honour, if awarded to her, might bring her way. Her only desire had been to derive as much fun as she could from the experience and return home to Summerhaze.

But the return journey to New Zealand and Summerhaze never happened. A twelve-month modelling contract had been offered to her and had promptly thrown her into a state of quandary. After a great deal of soul-searching and discussions with her mother, who had been with her, Romy had decided that it might be an experience too exciting to miss. And besides, a year was only a year . . .

'Five years,' she thought, staring at her reflection in the mirror. 'I haven't altered that much. Just matured a little, that's all.'

And indeed, the girlish roundness had been shed from her features, but all the same, she wouldn't have called herself gaunt. Admittedly there were hollows beneath her cheekbones and her neck was slimmer and her collarbones more pronounced, but her silver-green eyes were as clear and as frank as ever and her attractively shaped mouth sprang into a smile just as readily as it had always done.

On impulse, she decided to wind her thick strong hair up into a knot at the back of her head. She had spent no length of time anywhere where the sun was as strong or as plentiful as it was on the North Island's east coast, so to retain its lighter colour hadn't been possible except via artificial means. It was, as Nellie had said, darker and straighter than it had been and she didn't want to appear to her parents too unlike the Romy they had last seen. With the knot secured, she flicked at the short new hairs until they sprang in soft waves about her face, then reached for the plain gold loop earrings which she had tucked into a pocket down the side of her small cosmetic case.

CHAPTER TWO

AT a certain high point in the road Romy pulled over, stopped and climbed out of the car. Anxious though she was to get home, she was also extremely nervous. In fact the closer she drew to Summerhaze, the more tied and knotted up inside she became. What was it going to be like to see her parents and sister again after so long? What could she expect? Would the large gracious old homestead still be the same as she had left it? It had no doubt been treated to a new coat of paint by this time. Her mother had said in one of her letters a long time ago that it had needed repainting, but if she had mentioned in her letter what colours had been chosen, Romy couldn't remember what they were.

She stood at the verge of the road and shielding her eyes against the sun, looked out across the green rolling hills towards the vivid blue Pacific that could be seen in the distance. Beautiful. She lowered her hands and placed them both, fingertips meeting, across the small of her back and stretched, breathing in deeply as she did so.

What she had told Nellie had been true. Unbelievable though she could now consider it to be, she had forgotten the vibrance and richness of her own country, and the sweet smell of the sun-imbued earth which made her want to exclaim aloud with pleasure and hop the wire fence immediately before her and run and frolic in the grass just as the newborn lambs were doing. Come summer, she knew, the scene could well be a different one. In a matter of days the trees

could fade, their leaves droop, the grass could wither
and the hills would be scorched by a biting sun until
they resembled rugged golden shapes against a fierce
blue sky. Even so, its beauty would in no way be
diminished and the air would be as clear as crystal and
filled with the odours of the earth and the plant life it
produced.

There was no long driveway up to the homestead of
Summerhaze and during winter, when not shielded to
the same extent by the leaves of many deciduous trees,
the house could be seen fairly clearly from the road.
But privacy was and always had been assured, for
Summerhaze was the last property situated on a no-
exit road and traffic was virtually non-existent.

Romy quickly parked the car and climbed out, and
all at once it seemed as though she hadn't been nervous
at all, but this excited all along. She took a short cut
across the lawns beneath the spreading branches of a
sycamore tree just coming into leaf. Until her high-
heeled sandals came in contact with the flagstone path,
the only sounds to be heard were the birds, the distant
call of cattle and bleating of sheep and the jangling of
the bracelets on her wrists.

Her steps led her swiftly, automatically towards the
verandah, wide and sweeping, with a turret over the
corner entrance to the house. Once there she paused to
look out over the sloping lawns, dotted profusely with
clumps of daffodils, and slightly to the left, out through
and across the tops of trees to where the road and the
bay, a short distance on, could be seen.

The sound of footsteps came from within the house
and when she heard them proceed through the door
which opened behind her, she turned, slowly and even
a trifle apprehensively.

'Romy!'

Romy swallowed convulsively. 'Hello, Mum.'

'My dear God—Romy! Is it really you? I can't be-lieve it! We heard the car . . . I can't believe it. Matt! Julie!' In her excitement, Nina Palliser swung away to re-enter the house, then catching herself, turned back to hold out her arms to her daughter. 'Such a surprise!' she exclaimed, embracing her warmly and, with tears in her eyes, led Romy into the house. 'I can't believe it!' she exclaimed yet again, tightening the arm she had around Romy's waist.

'Oh, I'm here all right, Mum,' Romy laughed as they entered the dining-room, and gave her mother a hug to reassure her of her presence.

A single encompassing glance around the room revealed that there were several other people present besides Julie and her father, but right at that moment she had eyes only for her father, who was seated at the head of the dining table where he had always sat for meals. She saw him make to rise to his feet, his move-ments slightly slower and more careful than she re-membered them. But what shocked her more than this was the sight of his face—thin, the flesh loose and colourless, and his frame once so tall and straight, now spare and no longer emanating strength and vitality. He had always worked too hard, she thought, her eyes misting and she folded her arms about him. 'Hi, Pop.' She drew back and smiled at him tremulously.

'Well, well—Romy,' he said softly, giving the back of her neck a stroke and a pat. And he appeared too overcome at that moment to manage more than that.

Drawing back, Romy looked over at Julie, who had also risen from her seat at the dinner table. There was a fixed look of shock on her face, but as Romy stared at her she noticed that she had grown quite pale and that there was no sign of pleasure at all in her expression. Romy's heart sank. Were they never to be friends again? Not even after all this time? Longing to remind her of the love and warm camaraderie they had once shared, Romy rounded the table and put an arm about her sister. 'It's good to see you again, Lee.' She kissed her cheek. 'You're looking absolutely blooming.' She spoke the truth. Despite her present pallor, Julie looked the most attractive Romy had ever seen her. But it was no use. Her sister's shoulders remained rigid under her arm and her expression frozen.

'Hello, Romy,' she managed quietly between barely moving lips.

'Are you hungry, Romy? You must be, surely,' said her mother, not appearing to notice anything amiss between the sisters.

But then she never had, Romy thought fondly, treating her mother to a warm smile. 'Not really, Mum,' she said, dropping her arm. 'Just tired.' And for the first time she looked around at the two persons present besides her immediate family.

'You're so thin, you don't look as though you've eaten in weeks,' her mother was exclaiming. 'When did you arrive back? And why didn't you let us know? Surprises are all very well, but I nearly passed out with shock when I saw you . . .'

But Romy scarcely heard her. For the second time that day her eyes were caught and held by a pair of penetrating brown ones, and as she stared into them, she had the distinct feeling that those eyes had been on her and had never left her from the moment she had stepped over the threshold into the room. Her lips parted and she waited, almost expectantly, for the return of the sharp pleasurable pang that had divided her as she had stood at Nellie's front gate. But it never came. And instead of heat, she was aware of a vague chill creeping over her flesh. She felt pinned down under his gaze and although it was without expression, she sensed instinctively that he didn't approve of her. That he didn't approve of her one little bit.

Suddenly, aware that she was cringing before this stranger with a superior, condescending air, she rallied and forced herself to move forward with her hand outstretched. 'Hello,' she said, feeling her hand being taken very briefly by one a great deal larger, calloused and extremely dry. 'Quila, isn't it?'

'Please forgive our rudeness.' Matt Palliser, always the epitome of good manners, smiled apologetically at Quila and the younger man with him—a youth, really, Romy thought, smiling at him, for his clear blue eyes were resting on her as unwaveringly as Quila's were, but in a manner that differed from Quila's in every way. And when he smiled back at her, quickly and readily, albeit shyly, Romy thought to herself what a lovely boy he was—young, clean-cut and somehow innocent.

'How did you know who Quila was?' Matt had turned abruptly to his daughter.

'I popped in to see Nellie before coming out—I bumped into her nephew at the gate. We haven't been introduced. And I'd no idea he was coming on out here. Nellie never said.'

'Well,' Nina interposed brightly, 'this is Quila Morgan, your father's . . .'

'Summerhaze's manager,' Matt cut in suddenly. 'Despite what she says, Nina, I'm sure Romy's ravenous. If you fetch her something to eat, I'll perform the introductions.'

Romy looked at her father in surprise. She could never remember him ever having been so deliberately rude or brusque before, and certainly not to her mother. Her parents stood looking at one another and Romy noticed how pale her father looked, almost grey, and her heart squeezed with concern.

'Very well, dear,' Nina nodded. 'But sit down and finish your own meal before it grows totally cold.'

Matt turned his attention to Romy. 'Didn't Nellie explain to you about Quila?'

'Only that he was her great-nephew and that he'd recently returned from the States.'

'And that's all?'

'Yes, that's all. Why? Is there anything else? Some dark and gruesome secret?' Romy grinned impishly.

Matt's expression seemed to relax slightly. 'No. Only that about a year ago I assigned Quila to be Summerhaze's manager.' As he spoke, he turned his gaze on Quila. 'He's been a tremendous help to us.'

Quila's expression remained quite impassive.

'Quila, I'd like you to meet my youngest daughter, Romy. She's just spent five years in the States, so you'll probably find quite a lot to talk about.'

Summerhaze's manager? A manager on Summerhaze where there'd never been a manager before? Poor Pop! Romy's heart wrung with pity. Summerhaze had been farmed by Pallisers for three generations, and now, because her father's brother had died and his sons had sold their share to their uncle, and because her father had no sons himself, Summerhaze was to be managed by a stranger. 'How do you do?' She didn't proffer her hand again. And neither did she smile as she would have done had he done so.

'And this is his young friend, Leon, from the States. He's taking a year out to work here before returning home to go to university.'

'Hello, Leon.' She smiled again at the youth and extended her hand.

With slightly heightened colour, Leon took her hand briefly and murmured that he was pleased to meet her.

'Have you been here long?' Romy asked.

'Since July.'

'And from what part of the States?'

'My folks own a farm in the state of Iowa. Quila managed one of the neighbouring properties. That's how we met. Have you been to Iowa, Miss Palliser?'

'Call me Romy. And yes, I've been to Iowa, although only on a through visit, so I didn't get to see much. Most of my time was spent in New York and unfortunately I didn't see as much of the rest of the country as I would have liked.'

At that moment, Nina re-entered the dining-room and placed the plate she was carrying on the table and withdrew a table napkin and knife and fork from the drawer of the side table situated against the wall. 'I'll seat you here beside Julie, Romy. Now sit down, all of you, and finish your meal.'

'Mmm, it smells delicious,' Romy murmured, pulling a chair out from the table. She unfolded her table napkin and spread it over her lap. 'I didn't think I was hungry, but this is an aroma I haven't smelled in years.' And so saying, she threw a sideways smile at Julie, which was returned stiffly and with a marked lack of spontaneity and warmth.

'When did you arrive? And how much time are you able to spend with us?' Nina asked as soon as everyone had begun eating once more.

'I arrived in Auckland this morning and was lucky enought to get on the connecting flight to Wellington. I hired a car from there and here I am. I'm a free agent, so I can stay as long as I like.'

'But what about your work?'

'My contract is finished.'

'Weren't you offered another?'

'Oh, yes, but I thought it was time I came home for a while.' Romy's smile subsided a little as she turned her gaze on her father, who was sitting at the head of the table next to her. 'I should have come home sooner.' She put a hand over his which lay on the table beside his plate. 'I only found out recently that you hadn't been well. I wish you'd told me.'

He shook his head. 'There was no point in worrying you. You have your own life to lead, and that's how it should be. What is there for you to do back here?'

'I'm going to help you out on Summerhaze,' said Romy gaily, taking up her knife once more. 'Perhaps then you won't have any need for a manager.'

Her father laughed at this and Romy found her eyes drawn to Quila Morgan, who was sitting quietly eating directly opposite her. He didn't lift his gaze immediately, as though he knew she was expecting a reaction from him and so deliberately delayed providing one. When he did meet her gaze it was only briefly, dispassionately, then his eyes lowered to the well defined and painted outline of her mouth and dropped still farther to flicker over her braceleted wrists, ringed fingers and long painted nails. Not a muscle stirred in his face to bring into life any form of expression, or give away anything of what he might be thinking. He returned his attention to his plate and continued eating.

Without a word he had spoken volumes. He didn't like her, she thought. He really didn't like her. And this realisation caused her stare to become unblinking and rather bleak. But *all* men liked her, she told herself. They all responded favourably towards her—or had up until now. Why didn't Quila like her? What had she done . . .? Oh, well, what did it matter anyway?

It would happen sooner or later, as it had always happened whenever she had met for a second or third time men who, like Quila, had had the same tumultuous effect on her upon their first encounter. And so she studied him with a stare, distant and owning a trancelike quality that was induced by tiredness, and waited for the inevitable sense of disappointment to begin settling in. It never did. He wasn't handsome, but then good looks in a man had never attracted her. It was always a certain something that she had never been able to define and most of the men who had initially attracted her in the past had had that ingredient. But it wasn't very long afterwards that she discovered that the qualities which she could name and did look for were sadly absent. However, no one, no matter how much they might dislike the man, could say that Quila was soft or weak, for strength itself had gone into the designing of that attractively shaped mouth and moulding of his chin and the smooth brown column of his neck and self-possession was in every quiet line of him . . .

'Romy? Did you hear what your father said?'

At her mother's words, Romy's head swivelled around. She stared past her sister, vaguely noting her erect posture and mechanical manipulation of her knife and fork, and blinked slowly a couple of times. 'Sorry, Mum. What did you say?'

Nina smiled gently. 'You look as though you're about to fall asleep into your plate!'

Romy managed a faint grin and then passed a hand over her eyes as the room and everything in it began to tilt and sway. 'I think I really should go to bed.'

'Yes, that's a good idea.' Her mother rose to her feet

as she spoke. 'We have a lot of catching up to do, but it will be best left until you've had a good long rest. I don't expect you slept much during the flight.'

'No, not much. I never do.'

'I'll go and see to your room. It hasn't changed at all since you left.' And before Romy had a chance to assure her that she could make up her own bed, Nina was already on her way up the stairs.

Romy pushed back her chair and smiling at her father, she rose and leaned forward to kiss him. 'It's good to be home, Pop.'

'I'm glad you think so.' Matt caught her hand and gave it a squeeze. 'I think you'll enjoy the change—for a while at least.'

Romy shook her head. 'I must admit I was worried about coming back, but now that I am back, I know I wouldn't feel more content anywhere.'

What made her glance back over her shoulder just before she passed through the door, Romy had no idea. She couldn't even recall actually doing so and only realised that she had when her weary, heavy-lidded glance collided with Quila's. He had finished his meal and was leaning on his elbows and over interlocked fingers was watching after her somewhat absently. His gaze slipped in a downwards direction, resting momentarily on her slender feet and ankles shod in flimsy high-heeled sandals, then rose once more to meet hers. Quite bland though his expression was, Romy knew full well what was going on behind it. Well, he would keep, she thought without rancour, and climbed the stairs, yawning deeply.

Romy awoke from what had been a delicious sleep and lay still for several seconds in the fading light watching the long lace curtains billowing gently in the breeze and wondered where she was. There was no familiar traffic noise or wafting of unpleasant smells. Instead there was absolute silence and the air was fresh, cool and fragrant. She sat up with a start, saw her surroundings in full detail, then she remembered where she was and fell back on her pillow with a smile on her lips.

Home. In a room that was her very own with its double-hung sashcord windows, kauri ceiling and floorboards and old open fireplace. She glanced across at the fireplace, at its beautiful surround, ornately fashioned from kauri timber with an inset mirror panel on either side, deep rose ceramic tiles and brass fender. As a child she had loved Summerhaze's old fireplaces. Each one was different, and out of them all, she liked her own the best.

As a perfect foil for the rose ceramic tiles, the walls were papered in an old-fashioned pale green and on the bare varnished floorboards lay a large Chinese-cut carpet. The curtains were velvet and of the same dusky pink as the tiles, while the bedspread was white, like the curtains, and richly embroidered. The furniture in the room was also of kauri, with their various knobs, handles and hinges made of fashioned brass, and although the pieces of furniture were heavy, the room itself was big enough to accommodate and set them off to the best advantage. Across the top of a long and low chest of drawers sat her two dolls and several other well cherished toys, while her books lined the bookshelves exactly as she had left them five years before.

Resisting the desire to snuggle up in her comfortable three-quarter-size bed and drift off to sleep again, Romy pushed back the bedspread and slid out of bed. Clad only in her nightdress, she crossed to the window, pushed the bottom pane up farther and leaned out.

The smells exuded by a rejuvenating earth were, as evening encroached, many and varied. She breathed in deeply and wondered how it had been possible for her to have forgotten so much. The branches of a walnut tree were close enough for her to touch, and she thought back over the times she and Julie had, in the dead of a moonlit night, scaled along its branches and dropped on to the ground below and run down to meet their cousins at some appointed rendezvous point from where they would head towards the bay for a swim. How unfearing and irresponsible they had been, she thought with a smile. But they had been happier days.

She drew back from the window and reached for her dress and pulled it over her head. It was only when she sat on the edge of her bed and drew her sandals out from beneath it that she recalled the presence of two strangers at Summerhaze, and in particular the one who didn't much care for her. She looked down at the flimsy heel between her hands and knew without a shadow of doubt that Quila Morgan had passed judgment upon her. He considered her frivolous and without much substance—like these very sandals.

Romy pursed her lips thoughtfully for a moment or two. Then slipping on the sandals and brushing and tying back her hair, she left her room and made her way downstairs. The only sounds within the house were coming from the kitchen and these, plus the sudden melodic chimes from the old grandfather clock in the hall, told her that it was close to dinner time.

The door to the kitchen was on a spring-loaded hinge and it swung silently closed after she had passed through, to be greeted by smells of home cooking which she realised she had never fully appreciated before.

No major changes had been made to the kitchen, she

was swift to note, and she was pleased. She had always loved the old-fashioned atmosphere of the room, and to maintain it wasn't unpractical, even now, for the coal range was still used during the winter months when extra hot water was needed or as a cheap means to dry clothes, and also whenever there were visitors staying at Summerhaze whatever the season. And there was the high ceiling which often proved a blessing too, not only in winter when clothes were strung up on a rack to dry, but in the summer when the heat was intense.

It was a light kitchen and large, with vast cupboard space and plenty of room for the cumbersome Welsh dresser which was lined with crockery and china, its lower shelf cluttered with pads, letters, bills and note-books, plus pens, string, scissors and numerous other bits and pieces. The china had once matched, but as the set decreased owing to breakages over the years, patterns, shapes and sizes now varied greatly, and this Romy found pleasing and very homely.

A table was tucked away in one corner, old, solid and rustic, used by the family for breakfast and week-day lunches, surrounded by chairs with high carved backs and moulded legs. Above the head of the table was an old wireless, looking tired and worn but a proven faithful friend of her father's. Many an hour she remembered him having sat with his ear glued to it, listening to the races and the rugby and cricket broadcasts.

Nina had straightened from her task of rolling pastry out on her wooden worktable, white now from years of scrubbing its surface clean. She smiled at Romy and Romy thought her eyes looked suspiciously bright. Rounding the table, she gave her mother's shoulders a warm hug.

'I still can't believe you're home,' said Nina, curving an arm about Romy's waist and administering a squeeze while at the same time taking care not to touch her with her flour-coated hands.

'And I can't believe I *am* home. The house doesn't appear to have changed at all.'

'No,' Nina sighed. 'And not because there's nothing needing to be changed. It's an old house and requires a lot of upkeep.'

'But nothing too drastic. Built of kauri by pioneers—what more does it need to recommend it? It'll stand for ever.'

'Well,' Nina sounded a trifle dubious, 'let's hope so. Did you have a good sleep?'

'I don't think I'd call it sleep. I'm sure I just passed out, and I feel a lot better for it. What's the pastry for?' Romy asked.

'Your favourite—apple pie.' Nina reached for a tin and began to open it.

'What's this? Tinned apples? Don't we have an orchard any more?'

'The orchard's still there. I just haven't been bottling the way I used to. I was spoilt, I think, when you were here to do most of it for me.'

'With Pop falling ill the way he did, it must have been a big strain on you. Why didn't you let me know, Mum?'

'Your father wouldn't have it, and you know how stubborn he can be. When he digs his heels in, no one can shift him. Besides, I've had Julie, and she's been a tremendous support.'

But with not an ounce of love in her for this fine, character-loaded house or the land, Romy thought sadly. It was Julie who should have been born the so-called 'beauty' and won the contest and gone overseas to travel, broaden her horizons and mingle with the successful and sophisticated. She would have appreciated and revelled in such a life even more than Romy herself had. Instead, Julie had taken after their mother in looks and physique, being a slimmer version of the older woman, petite, with dark brown curly hair, generous mouth, pert nose and large brown eyes. At twenty-eight, she was an attractive woman, but she didn't have the winsomeness which Romy possessed and could well have done with a dash of her younger sister's more ebullient, outgoing nature. It was always said that Romy was a throwback from her father's side, which was an explanation Romy had shrugged at and accepted.

'How many hands does Summerhaze employ now?' she asked.

'I'm not sure exactly. About six or seven. There's always someone coming or going. I'm inclined to lose track.'

'And Quila Morgan?' queried Romy, broaching the subject casually. She sneaked a slice of apple from the tin.

'Your father explained about him, didn't he?'

'Summerhaze's manager. Summerhaze has never had a manager before—nor so many men.'

'I don't really think we can expect three or four employed men to do the same amount of work that Matt, Bob and the boys did, can we? As for Summerhaze never having had a manager—I suppose it's because we've never needed one before.'

Romy listened carefully to her mother's reply and was positive that she had deliberately injected a light note into her voice. 'How long has he been here?' she asked.

Nina frowned. 'Oh, about a year now, I'd say. But

surely you knew about Quila? I could swear your father wrote and told you he was employing extra help.'

'Yes, extra help, nothing about a manager.'

'Well, I expect he didn't want you to suspect that all was not well. He'd employed several other managers before Quila, so there's been a lot of new faces around here.'

'Why didn't the others stay?'

'For a variety of reasons. Either Matt wasn't pleased with their work or they didn't like it here.'

'Didn't like it here?' Romy frowned puzzledly. 'Who couldn't help but like it here?'

'Well, Quila likes it here and your father likes Quila, so for that we can be thankful.' And so saying, Nina pricked the top of the pie with a fork, then took the dish over and slid it into the oven.

'He doesn't stay in this house, does, he?' Romy gathered up the soiled utensils from the table and dropped them into the sink.

'No, no. The shepherd's cottage has been renovated and he lives there.'

'So why doesn't he eat there? Can't he cook?'

'He can cook and he does eat there, or with the other hands at their quarters, most of the time. But sometimes, at weekends especially, I like to invite him down for a meal or two.'

'Then he won't be dining here tonight?' Romy pressed, trying not to sound too hopeful.

'No. He and Julie had made arrangements to go into town together this evening.'

'He and—Julie?'

'Yes, and I'm beginning to suspect that Julie is quite attracted to him.'

'And is he attracted to Julie?'

Nina gave a sigh and reaching for the scraps of left-over pastry, began to re-roll it. 'I can only hope so. Quila's not an easy man to read. He's very interesting and very charming and makes good company, but he tells you only what he wants you to know. In that way he can be very canny . . .'

Charming? Romy was thinking wryly, listening to her mother absently and watching as she spooned jam into round pastry cases. She personally had encountered more charm emitting from fellow passengers on the New York subway at peak hour! She grimaced, then pointed to the tin of jam which her mother was holding. 'I can see I'll be jam-making soon as well as bottling.'

'Dear,' said her mother, looking at her with a grin, 'I hope so!'

Romy returned the grin. 'But right now I guess I'd be of more use if I set the table.'

In the dining-room, she spread a cream satin-finished cloth over the beautiful walnut table which was large and oval in shape and had a set of six matching chairs, all with tapestry-covered seats. From the walnut sideboard she selected three sets of cutlery, three place mats and three serviettes. Having positioned them on the table she paused in her task and gazed about her.

Allowing herself to be completely diverted, she wandered over to the pair of long windows which were both shaded by a majestic Japanese maple tree. In the winter, when the branches were bare and the sun was lower in the sky, the dining-room was lightened and brightened. In summer, however, when the branches were heavily laden, very little of the sun found its way into the room, so it proved a blissfully cool retreat sought when everywhere else was unbearable hot. The tree's miniature maple leaves were springing forth, profuse and yet delicate in appearance and turned an almost luminous chartreuse by the setting sun.

She remembered when they were children, how she and Julie had loved to play on and beneath this particular tree ... Why, the old rubber tyre they used to swing on was still there, hanging motionless alongside the trunk at the end of a now perished length of rope. Romy smiled. They had once had a proper swing, and a hammock as well. Benji, Julie's pet terrier, used to be housed in a kennel over further, by the hedge, but Benji had been run over by a tractor years ago and the kennel had been long gone. Yes, Romy thought, there had even been a time when grass had ceased to grow altogether beneath the Japanese maple. Now the entire area resembled a thick lush green carpet.

The door behind her opened and, thinking it was her mother who had come into the dining-room, Romy turned around slowly, after saying with a sigh: 'It's still as beautiful as I remember it.'

'You've only been here five minutes. You can't possibly tell.'

Romy's dreamy pleasure collapsed like a punctured balloon. 'Oh, hello, Julie. I thought you were Mum.'

Julie made no response and Romy began to feel a decidedly uncomfortable target of her sister's hostile, penetrating stare. Then: 'I must say you're looking as stunning as ever,' said Julie dryly, her eyes sweeping up over her younger sister.

Romy laughed and shrugged a little awkwardly. 'Nellie didn't think so. You should have heard her! Emaciated, she said I was—gaunt and with an unhealthy pallor. She couldn't have been more disapproving.'

The quality of Julie's stare and expression didn't alter. And again she was silent.

'Lee . . .' Romy began, almost in the form of a plea. Things between them simply had to change. This hostility had gone on for an entire year before she left Summerhaze. To carry it on over and, now, beyond five years was ridiculous.

'Why did you come back here?' Julie cut in, her voice low, yet like pure steel.

At that moment Romy was given an insight into the full extent of the enmity Julie harboured for her, and she was so stunned that even with the table set squarely between them, she felt almost impelled to take a step backwards. With difficulty she stood her ground and answered calmly: 'Because I learned that Pop was ill.'

'He's been ill for years now.'

'Then why didn't you write and tell me?'

'I wasn't aware that you didn't know.'

She was lying. The knowledge came to Romy in a flash, swift and sure. Suddenly she was angry and no longer had any desire to breach the ever-widening rift between them. 'You know very well that I had no inkling of Pop's illness,' she said coldly. 'Just what is up with you, Julie? Why didn't you want me to come home? And why is it you don't want me home now?'

Julie's face flushed a colour that matched the dress she wore, and if it wasn't for her rather contorted expression, she would have appeared extremely attractive with her hair, freshly washed, springing into shiny nut-brown curls about her face and her brown eyes sparkling with a brilliance that was born of health as well as a strange, inwardly corrosive anger. 'You really don't know, do you?' she all but spat, her fingers curling tightly around the sides of a chair. 'Oh, it's not just Dad's attention you win entirely for yourself, you've always done that. The minute you walked into a room where Dad happened to be you immediately won his undivided attention. No, it's not just Dad you manage to steal away from Mum and me, but everyone else as well. You walk into a room and wham! you've taken over. You did when you were eighteen, and judging by lunchtime's grand entrance and subsequent performance, you haven't changed.'

Romy had turned white and quite quite cold, capable only of standing exactly where she was, meeting her sister's venomous stare with her own confounded one.

'Oh, yes,' Julie gave a short mirthless laugh, 'you can look at me like that! And if you think I'm being eaten up by bitterness and jealousy, you'd be right. I am. I don't like myself for it, but that's the way things are. The happiest years of my life were when you were away, and you wonder why I didn't want you to ever come back. I gradually became Julie Palliser, you see, and ceased to be simply "Romy's sister".'

Romy was sickened and shaken to the very core of her being. Taking a deep breath, she forced herself to rally. She straightened her shoulders and tilted her chin and pressed her clammy hands against her sides. 'I'm glad—I'm glad that you decided to get this out into the open at last,' she said huskily. 'I was about sixteen or seventeen when I first noticed that you resented me, but I never knew just how much or realised that there were so many reasons why. But you speak as though I've spent my life deliberately devising this great conspiracy against you, as though I was an enemy. Good heavens, Julie, I can understand a certain amount of jealousy between us in our teens. They're competitive years for everyone, but you're now twenty-eight, an intelligent and very attractive woman . . .'

Julie's eyes flashed malefically and her lips tightened. She turned on her heel and made towards the door.

'Julie!' The sharp authoritative note in Romy's voice succeeded in apprehending her. 'I'm your sister, Julie,' she went on in a more subdued tone, 'I'd never do anything to deliberately hurt you. And if you don't know that, or refuse to accept it, then you've got even more of a problem than you realise. But Summerhaze is my home. Your parents are my parents. And I've as much right as you have to be here and I fully intend to stay. If either of us needs to change, then I'd say you do, and I suggest you do something about your attitude fairly quickly or else you'll lose out even more than you consider you already have. And remember this, Julie, if you do lose out somewhere while I'm home, then it'll be *your* doing, *your* responsibility—not mine.' Julie went ashen and Romy knew, with no sense of satisfaction, that a picture of Quila Morgan had risen before her mind's eye and that the pointed thrust she had made had gone home.

Unfortunately, the point couldn't have stayed sharp for long, because a dark sardonic expression began to creep slowly over Julie's features. 'You think you belong here, Romy, but you don't. You don't and never have!' One corner of her mouth lifted in what Romy suspected was supposed to be a smile. She left the room and Romy let her go, and the door shut with a decisive slam that told her that Julie was satisfied that she had delivered the final retort, laconic and absurd though it was.

The sun had set and the room was now quite dark, but Romy didn't notice. She discovered she was trembling slightly and so half sat and half leaned on the low narrow windowsill. All this time! she thought. All this time Julie had resented the love their parents had for her. They were proud of her, of the opportunities that had come her way and the subsequent success she had made of them. But they were no less proud of Julie when she attained her Diploma of Pharmacy and had found a job as manageress of one of Masterton's chemist shops. Why, she was doing a far more worthwhile job in life than Romy herself.

At eighteen, the only reason she had been able to come up with for her sister's attitude had comprised two words—Daryl Clarke, a young solicitor who, at the time of his entrance into their lives, had been aspiring to become a partner in his father's law firm.

At twenty-three, Julie had brought Daryl Clarke home for the first time. They had been seeing each other for some months and it was clear to anyone with half an eye that Julie was in love, seriously, for the first time in her life. Romy had no idea when she first noticed that the young man's attention had begun to stray in her direction, nor for how long he continued to date Julie in order that he could see her. Romy had done everything in her power to discourage him, from being deliberately absent when he visited the farm, or positively rude to him when to avoid him had been impossible. Strangely enough, her obnoxious behaviour towards him had only served to encourage rather than discourage him, and it had been only a matter of time before Julie had become aware of the situation.

Events such as these hadn't been exactly uncommon. Before Daryl Clarke, there had been a tendency in youths who wanted to date Romy to approach her via one who evoked in them less awe. The two sisters had had many a giggle over such episodes. But Daryl Clarke had been a different story. Daryl was the first and perhaps only man Julie had ever loved and over a man so unworthy, Romy believed that Julie had nursed a grudge against her ever since. However, it was clear now that Daryl had been only a part, a large part admittedly, but still only a part, that went into the making up of the whole of the reason for the stand Julie had taken against her.

'Romy?' Her mother came through the door that opened from the kitchen into the dining-room. 'What on earth are you doing, sitting there in the dark?' She switched on the light. 'Be a pet and come and help me serve up.'

'I'll be right there, Mum.'

It seemed, as far as Romy could determine, that the only enemy Julie possessed, outside of her own imaginings, was Julie, and as she pushed herself up and away from the window ledge, she sensed with a terrible certainty that Julie would never come to recognise or accept that fact.

CHAPTER THREE

WHEN Romy awoke the next morning, the sun was just rising; she could tell by the way the white curtains were tinged with pink. Quickly she slipped out of bed and crossed to the window and sure enough, although her window wasn't facing due east, the sun was casting its initial glow across the entire generous smattering of cloud. She breathed in deeply and could smell the rich earth, damp with dew, and the heavy fragrance of freesias, lilac and the jasmine and clematis that tumbled freely over the trellises she could remember her father having built and erected to her mother's specification when Romy was just a child.

How peaceful it was! And how at peace she felt. Catching up her towel and toiletries, she hurried along to the bathroom for a shower. The soap sprang into a lather, requiring no persuasion from her, and she revelled in the velvety feel of the rich lather and soft water on her skin again after so long.

Before breakfast she had re-acquainted herself with the entire front and back garden areas and was glad to see that the daffodils had been allowed to flourish and not mowed along with the rest of the vast sloping lawns. Having had to get accustomed to the confined living space of a New York apartment, she would never again take the luxury of the large spacious house with its sprawling tree-dotted gardens for granted.

She had always loved Summerhaze, but never with a passion as fierce as the one she felt now. How happy she would be if one day she was able to own this gracious old house with its gables and intricate fretwork, the lead-light panels set on either side of the front and side entrances. Most of all she delighted in the verandahs, deep and open, sweeping to follow almost the complete length of two sides of the house, its roof fashioning into a turret at the south-east corner. To one day marry a man who loved the land and shared her desire to fill Summerhaze's bedrooms with children had always been a cherished dream and one which had originated too far back for her to remember. Romy sighed. Where would she find such a man? There wasn't, and never had been, anyone on her horizon in whom she could show anything more than a fleeting interest.

Several days passed during which she did little more than talk, eat and sleep. It seemed that her capacity for all three activities had grown inordinately. At the end of each day that passed, she sensed with an increasing certainty that she had indeed done the right thing in following through that very hastily made decision to return home. That her parents were deriving great pleasure from her company and the stories she had to relate was undeniable, and she knew that she and Julie must settle their differences before the situation existing between them became obvious to their parents.

Perhaps it was the intoxication induced by being home again that had bemused her to such an extent that she had failed to notice from the very beginning just how run-down the house, the exterior in particular, and gardens had become in comparison with the pictures she had kept stored in her memory. What finally opened her eyes with a start was her first glimpse of the orchards situated to the rear of the back garden, behind the lawn tennis court. Even the sight of the neglected tennis court hadn't perturbed her to any great extent, but when she caught sight of the orchards, she then wondered why, for the court itself had never before been allowed to get so overgrown. While sometimes, following the summer, certain areas of the high wire fencing had been lost to sight by a notorious rapid-growing creeper, that same creeper had always been dealt with before the arrival of the next tennis season. Now, as things were, she doubted if she would be able to find the entrance gate. She did, however, only to find it necessary to quickly turn her back on the sight of the long coarse mixture of weed, grasses and thistles, and the tennis net, perished and hanging in tatters.

The orchard was large and had always been devoted only the minimum amount of time and attention, yet it produced faithfully year after year. Pruning had been one chore which had been executed without fail every year, while spraying had always been a rather hit-and-miss affair and sheep had been brought in at intervals to keep the grass down. Now the entire area was covered in a tangle of undergrowth that would require a scythe to remove it and the trees themselves looked as though they hadn't been tended for years. As Romy gazed upon the sight, she wondered about the fruit, what happened to it and what quality the trees now produced. They were old trees, admittedly, nevertheless she was sure that a lot of the fruit would be salvageable and certainly could be bottled or made into jam. It sickened her to entertain the possibility, the very real possibility, that the fruit was being allowed to fall from the trees and left to lie and rot in the grass.

In something of a daze, Romy turned away and retraced her steps back through the long grass, made sodden by the preceding night's rainfall. It seemed a deserted area, as though no one ever bothered to come here now, she thought. As though they had forgotten its very existence. And yet it was not very far at all from the back boundary of the garden.

Then as she walked, deep in thought and the fingers of her hands poked into the shallow pockets of her fashionable tweed jacket, it came home to her suddenly that her mother was no longer as young as she still featured in Romy's memories of her, and as a consequence, she couldn't possibly possess the same energy and verve. And the worry of her husband had been an added burden and a monstrous one at that, with its own particular toll to exact.

As for Julie—well, Julie's interests never had lain at Summerhaze. Occasionally she had brought her friends home to play tennis or to swim in the river that ran through the property, but those occasions had been rare and had become fewer still when she discovered the attention they had been inclined to heap upon her younger sister. No, Julie had at a relatively early age learned to cultivate an interest in city dwellers and in activities that were usually carried out in the city rather than those closer to home.

Upon drawing near to the house, Romy deliberately slowed her pace and tried to view the scene before her more objectively than she had been doing since her arrival home. The house hadn't been painted during her absence after all, she realised with an abrupt shock. The once cream paint was now white, chalky and flaking off in numerous large patches, particularly noticeable when looking towards the upper regions of the house. The green of the eaves and the corrugated iron roof were also fading and naked timber and iron were becoming visible. Upon closer inspection the garden, though beautiful and colourful, was undisciplined, and although the lawns were obviously mowed regularly, the edges were no longer kept in the trimmed tidy condition she remembered.

A lump had begun to form in Romy's throat. Things really did change. She had never really seen, or if she had, recognised, evidence of change taking place before. Of people growing older, more frail, having to cope with illness that restricted activity and sapped their strength.

Long before she had left Summerhaze, the sixteen-hundred-acre farm had been owned jointly by Matt and his older brother, Bob. Bob, a widower, had lived with his two sons in a house he had built on the property at the edge of the southern boundary in a direct line with Summerhaze. The right to live in the family homestead had been his, but his wife had indicated that her preference was for a new house, so the homestead had come to Matt. Work on the farm had always been a combined effort—Matt and Romy and Bob and his two sons, Kit and Sean. Romy had loved pitching in with the four males and had never thought of herself as being a sex apart. She rode just as well as any of them and had proven just as indispensable when it came to each and every one of the chores that had needed to be tackled.

But in just a few short years, all that had changed. Bob had been knocked over and killed by a drunken driver only days before Romy's seventeenth birthday. Sean had been away at university at the time and a short while after the tragedy announced his intention not to return to farming. It had been only a matter of three years after this that Kit, the elder by six years, also decided not to continue but to sell Matt both his share of Summerhaze and the share he had been in the process of purchasing from his brother and try a new life in Australia. Matt had failed in his attempts to persuade his nephews to reconsider the decisions they had made, and only now was Romy able to glean some insight into just how grieved and heartsick her father must have been.

Slowly yet decisively she altered her direction and began to head towards the track which would in turn take her up to where Quila Morgan and the men who had been hired to work for her father were housed. The distance between the homestead and the shepherd's cottage was approximately a mile and the shearers' quarters, which, she had learned, had been turned over to the other more permanent employees such as shepherds and farm labourers, were situated a short distance farther on.

As she walked, the spring sun, sloping through clouds that had shed their rain the night before, lay like a warm mantle across her shoulders and the blue leaves of the gum trees and the leaves sprouting forth from the beeches and poplars which haphazardly lined both sides of the track shone and presented a beautiful sight. But Romy was only half aware of each of these two features of her walk, and it was only as she neared the men's dwellings that she raised her eyes from the track, drying slowly in the morning sun, and took stock of her surroundings.

What her mother had told her was true. The shepherd's cottage had not long been renovated. The men's quarters had also been altered slightly, extended and painted. Beyond these dwellings stood the implement sheds and stables and between the two lay several corrals. In the distance was the familiar sight of the shearing sheds and numerous sheep pens standing within a framework of weeping willows, oak and poplar trees. The entire picture seemed to be set against the green and pastel blue of near and distant hills, while directly behind her the ocean was more clearly visible than it was from the homestead and so vibrantly blue it almost hurt the eyes to look on it. How beautiful it all was! How fresh, bright and clean, smelling as newly washed as it looked, with the bleating of sheep and the ceaseless chatter of birds and the call of the magpies and various insects the only sounds to be heard.

Then, suddenly, another sound, the sharp ear-splitting explosion of a rifle shot, rang out, shattering the peace and causing Romy to almost jump out of her skin. When the last echo died away, all was quiet, uncannily so, for the insects and birds had fallen silent. Reacting finally, Romy began to run, swiftly towards the corral from where she suspected the shot had come.

Upon rounding the men's quarters, from where she could see the corrals clearly, she came to an abrupt halt. 'Rangi!' The name was whispered in disbelief and her heart, which had been beating so madly, seemed to stop altogether. Slowly she continued on until she was able to take the upper rung of the high fence in her hands, and stared aghast at the sight of her father's favourite gelding lying on its side on the floor of the corral.

Without pausing to think, she climbed the fence, jumped down into the corral and started towards the horse's rump, its coat glinting auburn in the sun. She didn't see or, more correctly, failed to register the sight of a small group of men standing with several feet separating them some distance from the animal's head. All she was intent on was reaching the animal for whom her father had harboured a very special fondness for as far back as she could recall.

At that point, she heard a shout. What happened after that she wasn't exactly sure. It was all so sudden.

Something that felt like a steel band seemed to clamp on to her waist, winding her, sending her reeling physically as well as with fright. Her feet flailed, tripped over some obstacle and she fell with a resounding thump and the wind burst from her body on a startled yell. No time was had to regain her breath before a heavy weight came crashing down on top of her. Stunned, she could do nothing other than stare up, almost sightlessly, into the angry face of Quila Morgan looming directly above her own. His weight bore down on her only momentarily, for as suddenly as it had fallen upon her, it lifted and she felt herself hauled to her feet, shaken with suppressed violence, then released.

'You little fool!' the man exclaimed. 'What the hell did you think you were doing?'

White and shaken, Romy's gaze became unriveted and slipped beyond his face to follow the direction in which he was gesturing to where the horse, though dead, lay still kicking spasmodically.

'Didn't you realise you could have been seriously injured?'

'I—I'm afraid I—didn't think.'

'You didn't think! Is it possible that you've got even less sense than I gave you credit for?'

At that, Romy's gaze swung back to his, her attention totally won away from the horse. She had started to tremble with reaction and one side of her body was beginning to throb from its violent encounter with the ground. 'Have you forgotten who you're speaking to?' she tried to upbraid him, but failed miserably, for her voice shook and her eyes had grown suspiciously bright.

'I haven't forgotten,' Quila assured her grimly. His eyes swept over her and even though she could detect no evidence of contempt in his regard, she was none-theless sure it was contempt for her that he was feeling. 'If you must keep appearing where you don't fit in, dress for it! You're not on the modelling circuits now!'

And by the time Romy had looked up from inspecting the puddle she had just fallen into and the resultant grazing of her soft leather shoes and the muddy stain which had spread along the thigh of her beige linen slacks and up over the back of her jacket, Quila had rejoined the men, who had stood watching the entire spectacle with both interest and curiosity.

Romy turned away and, with hands not quite steady, she re-coiled her hair, then swung herself back over the corral fence. The male laughter she heard following her departure didn't perturb her unduly. She was too busy pondering on what was upsetting her the most—to have seen the once proud and beautiful Rangi lying on the ground, shot to death, or Quila's manhandling of her. However, if he hadn't manhandled her the way he had, she realised now, there could have been dire consequences. One strike from a shod hoof would have done her considerably more harm than the fall she had suffered. What on earth had she been thinking of, to have run towards the horse the way she had done? That she should have known better there was no question. She sighed.

What a strange man Quila Morgan was, she mused. It was as if he had decided to take an instant and per-sonal dislike to her. 'And he doesn't even know me,' she thought. Or perhaps he behaved like that with everyone he first met. She shrugged. She hadn't met anyone—well, any male—quite like him before. There had certainly been a number of females who had shown a ready willingness to dislike her on sight.

It was only as she arrived back at the homestead that

she realised she hadn't confronted Quila with what was on her mind. Which meant another trek up there later. Her mind baulked slightly at the thought of it. Not today, she decided, and went upstairs to change out of her soiled clothes.

Only Romy and her mother sat down to lunch that afternoon, and Romy was rather glad, since it meant that without her father present she could ask her mother some pertinent questions, and the opportunity to do so arose immediately and was provided by her mother.

'There's only the two of us lunching today,' she said, slipping a patchwork tea-cosy over the teapot. 'Your father's gone into town.'

'Oh? What for? Anything special?'

'He needs one or two odds and ends in the tool line. The garden's been worrying him for a long time and now that the weather is beginning to pick up, he wants to spend some time doing a few of the chores he's had to let go.

'The vegetable garden looks okay,' commented Romy.

'Yes, between us we've managed to keep that up. It was the most important.' About to pour the tea, her mother paused and looked up. 'I've made tea for both of us out of habit. There's coffee, though, if you'd prefer it.'

'No, I never adopted the Americans' penchant for coffee. Tea will suit me fine. Does Pop also mow the lawns?'

'No, Quila sends one of the lads to do them once a week.'

'And that's all?'

'Yes, Matt doesn't ask him for more than that.'

'*Ask* him? Why does Pop need to *ask* him for anything? Surely as manager he does as Pop instructs him to do?'

'Have you begun to take sugar in your tea nowadays?' asked her mother, suddenly digressing as she noticed Romy dipping a spoon into the sugar basin.

'No, I don't have sugar normally. It's just that I had a bit of a shock this morning and I still feel a little shaky at the knees.' In answer to her mother's worried querying look, Romy told her briefly what had happened.

'Your father knew Rangi was to be put down,' Nina explained when Romy had finished. 'He knew Rangi was going lame and did all he could for him. But it was no use. So he asked Quila to put him down and let him know when it was done.'

Romy sighed. It was a deep, rather troubled sigh. 'How things change—how they *have* changed,' she amended, looking up from the open salad sandwich she was making.

Nina smiled. 'We're just getting older, Romy, that's all—Rangi, your father and me, and this house. We've all weathered, and some of us not very well.'

'Yes, I've discovered—about the house, I mean.'

'Ah, so you've come down to earth enough to notice!' Nina laughed.

Romy grinned in response. 'Has it been so obvious?'

'That you've been floating along on Cloud Nine for the past few days since you've been home? Yes. I was hoping you'd last up there a good while longer so that you wouldn't want to leave for a long time yet.'

'I don't want to leave for a long time, Mum. Not for a very long time.' Romy leaned across, took her mother's hand and gave it a gentle squeeze. 'I'm loving being back.'

'But for how long? For how long, Romy?'

'I want to stay. I don't want to go anywhere ever again. I'd love to stay right here. It's . . .' She hesitated, withdrew her hand and sat back in her chair. 'It's just that I couldn't bear to see how overgrown the garden was, and the tennis court and orchards. They look as though no one has ever set foot there. And the house used to look so proud and happy and bright. Now, with the paint peeling off, it looks so sad. That's why I went up to the cottage, to have a word with Quila and see if he couldn't spare a few men to help tidy the place up a bit . . .'

'Oh, no, Romy,' her mother cut in quickly. 'I don't think that would be a very good idea.'

'But why not? Even if they could just do the very heavy work, I could manage the rest.'

'Really, Romy, I don't think your father would agree to that. And I'm positive Quila wouldn't. I can't see him consenting to something like that at all.'

Romy looked a trifle bewildered. 'I don't really think Quila has much choice in the matter, Mum.'

At this, Nina appeared to be somewhat discomfited. 'Romy, I honestly think things are best left as they are. After Kit and Sean pulled out of Summerhaze, your father had to work a great deal harder, and it was only to be expected that the jobs around the house had to be let go.'

'But didn't he hire some men? He wrote and told me that he'd taken on a shepherd and several labourers.'

'And so he had. Only he should have done that right from the beginning, but he was worried about the finances, having had to buy their share of the property from Kit and Sean. I think the worry and the extra work took their toll. It was really touch and go there for a while, Romy. The men he hired weren't up to much, not when comparing them with Bob and the boys. Finally we were forced to fire them and bring in the stock and station agents to buy most of the stock we had to pay some of our debts. We even thought we might be forced to sell up altogether. Then Quila arrived. He's been a lifesaver, Romy.'

But Romy couldn't have cared less about Quila Morgan.

A lump seemed lodged in her throat. She gazed at her mother beseechingly. 'Why, *why* didn't you let me know?' Her hand resting on the table curled into a fist. 'I could have helped. I could have come home. I had money just sitting in a bank over there—doing *nothing*!'

'Can you see your father doing that, Romy? Asking you to come home? Taking your money? Can you? No, of course not. He wouldn't have dreamed of it. And you mustn't let on to him that I've told you all that I have. He doesn't want you burdened down by his problems. There's time enough ahead of you to have to confront the problems of life. Right now he considers you should be out and enjoying life, finding someone to settle down with, and I agree with him.'

'And did you—when you thought you might lose him?'

'No. But I respect him and I respected his wishes. There's no need for you to worry, Romy. Your father feels he can trust Quila as much as he did his own brother. Quila's getting the farm on to its feet again, building up the stock and upgrading the pasture and general maintenance. He knows what he's doing and he's hired several reliable men to help him. I doubt that he'll let any of them go to do the work required to be done around here.'

Privately, Romy continued to disagree. She also had

a niggling suspicion that her mother was keeping something back from her, but when she searched her mind for some solid foundations on which to base her suspicion, she couldn't come up with even one. 'Mum, I want you to promise that you'll tell me if there are any financial problems . . .'

'There aren't, Romy. Things were a bit tight when Sean wanted to pull out and then Kit a short time later. Matt had to take out a loan to buy their shares or face the prospect of splitting and selling half of the property.'

'What's happened to their home?'

'The Meadows? It was sold, along with a block of about a hundred acres, to a couple who want to farm a smallholding and become self-sufficient.'

For a short period Romy lapsed into a thoughtful silence, automatically eating the food on the plate in front of her. Then after a while, she commented: 'There's a lot of citrus fruit going to waste in the orchard, Mum—not to mention the tamarillos.'

'Well, Romy, look at it this way: there are two things going for it. Number one, you're home, and number two, this time around there'll certainly be no shortage of jam or preserving jars.'

Romy laughed, 'Only seals!'

'Only seals.'

'I suppose with so much on your plate these last few years, you haven't continued our tradition of holding an annual picnic for the I.H.C. children?'

'Goodness, no!' Nina's eyes widened in amazement. 'Do you know, I'd forgotten all about those picnics. What a chaotic time they were! And I'm ashamed to admit that we haven't held, or even thought of holding one since you left.'

'Oh, Mum!'

'Well, you were the chief organiser. Who, apart from you, would be game enough to volunteer?'

'Do you think we can start again this year?' Romy's eyes lit up. She began peeling an orange. 'I'll assume full responsibility—financial and otherwise,' she added quickly, swift to note her mother's slight hesitation. 'I'll enjoy it.'

'But who are you going to get to help you? Sean and Kit did so much of the heavy work, setting up trestles, transporting the food and putting up decorations. And what about the organising of the games? I doubt whether Julie has grown any more enthusiastic about such things over the past five years.'

Romy winked. 'Just leave it to me!'

'If you think feminine wiles are going to work on Quila Morgan, I think you're going to be very much mistaken.'

'Why? Hasn't he any imagination?' Her mother laughed. 'From what I've seen of him so far, I'd say he hasn't. Not much humour, either. But don't worry, Mum. I don't think I'm the sort to use feminine wiles. I intend merely to ask him to lend me a hand—or two.'

'Romy . . .'

'Mmm,' Romy responded, squinting and sitting up sharply as a well-aimed squirt of orange juice caught her in the eye.

'Oh, nothing. It's not important.'

But it was as if a flash of timely intuition told Romy immediately, even before she had asked, what was on her mother's mind. 'I know Julie cares for him, Mum. And I've never yet wanted or cared for any man she's ever set her sights on. You know that.'

'Yes, yes, I do know that, and I've never believed otherwise. Only this time . . . Well, Quila's a man, and in no way like the boys who visited Summerhaze five years ago.'

'I know, Mum. And there's another difference too. This particular man doesn't much like this particular woman. And take it from me, I can live without his approval or appreciation!'

Nina laughed and sighed. 'Didn't you ever meet anyone you could care for? Not in all this time?'

'Not even one.' Romy made a rueful face and flexed her sticky fingers. 'But don't fret—I'm happy enough single.'

'For now,' Nina returned, apparently determined to have the last word.

CHAPTER FOUR

THAT evening, Romy took pleasure in dressing for dinner. She hadn't seen her father all day and she knew it was a treat for him to see her appearing at dinner looking fresh and attractive. She coiled her hair, which had succumbed quickly to its exposure to sunlight and was already beginning to lighten, into a loose knot at the back of her head and, after slipping her set of gold bracelets on to her wrist and fixing her wide gold semi-circular earrings, she stood back to view her reflection.

Her bare legs were long and slim and her feet looked even more shapely in the wedged-heeled backless sandals. The pale cool green of her dress suited her perfectly and the softly gathered material slipped and swirled about her legs as she walked. A wrap would probably be required for later, for her arms and neck were bare and evenings were still inclined to grow cool as the nights wore on. She pursed her mouth, painted the same colour as her nails, and noticed that already her face was faintly tanned. She would soon need to change the tone of the cosmetics she used, she thought inconsequentially. And half way down the stairs, she grimaced as she suddenly recalled the freckles that had been blissfully absent during every one of the five summers she had been out of the stronger sunlight of home.

Upon entering the lounge, she found her father where he usually was, seated in his favourite deep-studded Winchester leather armchair. However, she didn't expect to see Quila at all, much less seated by him with an ice-cold lager near at hand. She recovered quickly, though she was unable to tell whether it was an agreeable or disagreeable surprise to find him there.

'Hello, Pop.' She went across and kissed her father soundly on the cheek, and could tell he was pleased and that he was proud of her by the way he took her slim hand in his and gripped it tightly. It was times such as this that made her glad that she had made the extra effort to look especially nice.

She straightened and looked over at Quila who, at her entrance, had risen from his chair. She acknowledged him with a smile and returned the greeting but not the smile. 'Am I intruding?' she asked, her question directed at both men.

'No,' said her father with gratifying swiftness, 'not at all. Would you like a drink?'

He made to rise, but Romy forestalled him by laying a hand on his shoulder. 'I'll get myself a drink. You stay there.'

It took only a few seconds to discover that in the drinks cabinet there was not such an array as there used to be. Not much to choose from at all—port, brandy, sherry and beer and several varieties of soft drink. Just one more thing at Summerhaze that was not as it once was. But Romy made no comment and didn't hesitate over her choice. She poured a small sherry and returned to her father's side and with an uncontrived elegance, sat on the curved arm of his chair.

After a moment or two she looked up at Quila over her sherry glass. Matt was talking to him and Quila, though no doubt listening and taking in every word, was staring intently at the marks his fingers had made on the frosted sides of his glass.

The two men conversed together at some length, and

after a while Romy became acutely conscious of the studiousness with which Quila avoided looking at her. And of course he never spoke to her at all.

'Well,' said her father, when there came a lull in their conversation, 'what do you think of my beautiful daughter?' He placed an arm about her waist.

This should prove interesting, Romy thought, suppressing with considerable effort all outward manifestations of her mirth. She leaned nonchalantly on her father's shoulder and finally felt what it was like to be the target of those expressionless brown eyes.

'She certainly is pleasing to look at,' was Quila's very measured reply.

Matt laughed. 'I get the feeling that that was what's called a loaded response!'

And how, thought Romy wryly. 'Actually, I came to see you this morning,' she said aloud, straightening in her position on the arm of her father's chair, 'to ask a favour of you.'

The deadpan expression which had come over Quila's face upon her entrance into the room didn't lift when he returned his attention to her. There was an air of resignation about him, as though he had finally conceded that to continue to avoid speaking to her indefinitely was not going to be possible. In fact, Romy was sure that if it were not for her father's presence, he would have excused himself long before this. She felt a nameless prickle which continued for some time before revealing itself to be vague irritation. She mused upon it absently. Really, it was beginning to pall, being on the receiving end of all this groundless animosity.

'I'm not at all sure that Quila will be able to spare any help, Romy,' said her father when she had told Quila the original purpose of her visit. 'Spring's a busy time.'

'I hadn't forgotten,' Romy assured him, patting his arm. 'But I saw quite a number of men up there this morning. Surely one can be spared for a week or two. After that, I'm sure I could manage all the rest that needs to be done.' She looked back at Quila once more and saw that his gaze was resting on the slender white hand that lay on her father's arm, taking in the rings on three of her fingers, the bracelets that jangled on her wrist whenever she moved and, last of all, her long painted, impeccably manicured nails. Almost before she realised it, his eyes had lifted and were now staring into hers. For a split second she was given a glimpse behind the mask and saw a truth there that made a feeling, a nausea, spring up from the pit of her stomach to the base of her throat. His eyes were suddenly blank once more, but she knew with a certainty that what she had seen in them had been intense dislike and— utter repugnance. The dislike she might wonder at, but with that at least she could cope. But why should the sight of her hands repel him? She had beautiful hands. They had been sought after for many an advertisement.

Involuntarily, her gaze dropped to the hand still resting on her father's arm, only to find that of their own volition her fingers had curled up into her palm and out of sight. She straightened them again immediately. Really, who was this man that she should allow him to intimidate her like this? Overseas, men had fallen over themselves to win her attention. There had been men who would have given her anything she asked. This fact had never impressed her, rather she had considered her abilities in this respect somewhat vulgar and futile and the behaviour of her suitors, when not amusing, irksome and a constant source of embarrassment. And yet here she was now recalling this same knack she had denounced and experiencing definite umbrage that she wasn't having the same effect over this man which would cause him to behave towards her in a manner she so despised.

'Anyway, there's no need for Quila to have to go one man short,' Matt was saying. 'I went into town today to see about hiring some up-to-date equipment and getting out in the garden myself.'

These words effectively dispelled Romy's pre-occupation. Her bowed head shot up, but before she could protest Quila was saying calmly: 'There's no need for that, Matt. I can let young Leon go for as long as he's needed. I'm sure he won't mind helping out down here.'

And while her father considered this proposition, and decided that Leon would be the ideal person for the job and thanked Quila for suggesting it, Romy gazed at Quila in puzzled silence, wondering who this man was that he should address her father, his employer and senior by at least twenty-five years, by his Christian name, and how it was that such a personal footing came to be arrived at in the first place.

At that moment the door to the lounge opened and Julie came in. Romy had glanced up casually, then straightened, sensing the inevitable need to brace herself, a ritual which she found necessary to carry out whenever she and her sister came face to face.

Julie's glance was swift and all-encompassing. When it came to rest on Romy, full of accusation, Romy knew that in her sister's mind she was sketched in as the author of a conspiracy to ensnare and carry off her and the family's much admired and favoured prize, Quila Morgan.

'I'm sure Julie comes bearing mother's invitation to you to stay to dinner, Quila,' said Matt.

'Yes, you're right, Dad. Would you like to stay?' Julie looked at Quila and the expression in her eyes caused a feeling akin to pain to assail Romy and she wanted desperately to avert her gaze, but couldn't. 'We're having a roast which is guaranteed to beat Pete's or your cooking any day.'

'Thanks, Julie, but not tonight, if you don't mind. I've promised Leon a game of chess and I somehow think it'll be an all-night affair.' Quila gave her a slight apologetic smile which had come and gone before Romy had had time to register the change, if any, the small fleeting smile had made to his features. As he drained his glass, she transferred her gaze to Julie once more and was in time to catch the full benefit of the virulent glare she flung in her direction before turning abruptly and leaving the room.

Romy remained behind as the others left the lounge and wandered across to the windows that faced towards the north-west. Like those which faced north-east, the windows reached almost to the floor, but unlike the others, access could be gained via these to the verandah and from there one could look out over towards the jutting arm of hills which enclosed the bay and now lay basked in the last of the day's sunshine.

To her way of thinking, Quila was a strange man, and as her mother had already observed, a man who gave nothing much away. She was probably the only member of the family who could claim to find him not exactly prepossessing, even unlikeable, but she was nevertheless quite positive that no one could make the mistake of judging him and describing him as stupid. No, she suspected he was an astute man, one who had seen and experienced a great deal. Therefore it only stood to reason that he must know how Julie felt about him. Did he reciprocate those feelings? And if he didn't and yet was still prepared to offer Julie marriage, would she accept him without love? Why, he could be entertaining this very moment the notion of capitalising on Julie's love for him and Matt's trust and obvious admiration in order to become the heir to Summerhaze!

But was there any real danger? Was there any valid reason to fear that she might lose all rights she now enjoyed, to live on Summerhaze and to look upon it as her home? Especially when she knew how, in her heart, Julie hated Summerhaze and would never agree to living out her life there without putting up a fight and utilising every weapon at her disposal.

The racing content and direction of Romy's thoughts caused her to bite down hard on the nail of her forefinger until one of her front teeth pierced through its brownish-pink enamel coating. She knew her sister and was well acquainted with her attitude towards Summerhaze, but Quila Morgan was an altogether different and more complex character. She brought her hand down and appeared to be examining the damage when all the while she was seeking to find the answer to the most crucial question she had asked herself so far. Was Quila Morgan really to be trusted? She intended to find out, and was determined not to allow his personal and obviously antagonistic feelings for her to influence her final analysis.

And so later that evening, when they had a moment to themselves, Romy informed her father of her intention to go out with Quila on his rounds of the farm and discover and judge for herself whether or not he was worth all this approval and heartfelt admiration.

'To spy on him, you mean!' her father exclaimed, totally averse to her plan from the start.

'To supervise, Pop, not spy,' Romy remonstrated him teasingly.

'The same thing,' he insisted.

'But, Pop, what does it matter? I won't let on to him that you know anything about it. That'll let you out. As for him—he's only another hired hand in a sense, and for a hired hand he's ingratiated himself pretty deeply into this family. I'll bet there's a lot about him you don't know.'

'I know all I need to know. He has exceptional references and he's a man. He knows how to conduct himself like a man, and that's a pretty rare quality these days.'

'You mean he's got a firm handshake and he can look you in the eye?'

'Among other things. Now look here, my girl,' her father went on, endeavouring to appear tough in the face of her mischievous banter and determination to win him around as she usually succeeded in doing, 'you can put your organisational abilities to work in some other direction. You're no longer a tomboyish teenager. Farming's a man's work—stay out of it and let Quila and his men get on with their work the way they think fit.'

'But how do you *know* he's all you think he is? He could be putting it across you. It is possible, you realise? No, I won't rest until I've seen for myself and can report back.'

'Then if you get sent on your way with a flea in your ear, don't come complaining to me!' Matt huffed in sheer exasperation, both with her and his failure to enforce his will. 'I won't have one iota of sympathy for you.'

'Oh, Pop, you have no faith in me. Don't you think I know how to handle men by now? I certainly should do, I've had plenty of experience over these past five years.'

'Not with men like Quila, you haven't.'

This time it was Romy's turn to huff. 'You know, the trouble with you and Mum is that you're both determined to have the last word!'

'And your trouble is you're too determined and used to having your own way!'

Romy raised an eyebrow at him. 'See what I mean?' And so saying, she spun gracefully around on one foot and left the room, closing the door firmly behind her.

He was right, of course, she realised, standing on the other side of the door. She hadn't had much experience of men of Quila Morgan's sort, which she hadn't counted as any loss up until now. But even so, the experience of men which she had had must surely stand her in good stead, and despite the impression she had given her father, that she was confident of her abilities, she was in no way reckless or pushy in her dealings with others, even when they did come under the category of "employee".

The next morning Romy rose early, showered and dressed in a pair of loose-fitting khaki slacks and a light sleeveless red, cream and gold patterned khaki blouse. She slipped a pair of flat sandals on to her feet, cast aside all jewellery, tied her hair back into a knot, removed her nail varnish and then unemotionally sat down to cut and file her nails until they were the shortest they had been in five years. She didn't linger in her inspection of her hands when she had finished. One glance was enough to reveal that they looked almost as square and capable as they had been before she left for overseas. And with the work that now awaited her, it wouldn't be long before they were just as brown and just as tough.

She skipped breakfast, because she wanted to make

sure that she caught Quila before he had finished his.

Despite the hour, the sun was hot and beat down on her as she walked quickly up towards the men's quarters. By the time she had arrived, perspiration had gathered down her back and across her brow. She was by no means fit. After a few days of manual labour she would be sore and as stiff as a board!

There was no garden whatsoever around the men's quarters and the lawns were roughly cared for and so worn away in patches that in some places the patches were actually larger than the areas of lawn. Instead of crossing at the little wooden bridge, Romy jumped down the narrow creek which for some distance ran parallel with the track, and crossed the lawns via the concrete path and not by one of the many tracks worn across them.

There was a great deal of clanging and banging, loud and bawdy talking, and many bursts of unrestrained laughter coming from within the quarters, which took Romy right back seven or so years to when she was home and the shearing gangs came to stay on Summerhaze. She stopped for a moment and listened, enjoying the nostalgia that the sounds and the smell of fried breakfasts brought rushing back.

Her reminiscences were interrupted almost before they had time to begin as one or two of the voices drifting to her came closer and more distinct, causing her to realise that a couple of the men had moved to the window which was situated near her head. Instinctively she ducked back and to one side, then made to move away in the direction of the front door, when the content of their conversation drew her back.

'Do you think she looks as good in real life as she does in those pictures?'

'How could I tell?' came an English-accented reply.

'I was standing as far away from her as you were. Right next to you, you burk.'

'Well, if she does, she'd sure do me.'

'It's amazing what they can do with a little bit of paint. It hides a multitude of sins and in most cases a bad complexion.'

'Is that for real? No, I can't believe that. It's amazing, isn't it, how she can look like an angel in one picture and so darn sexy in another.'

'Oh, give it a rest, Bimbo!'

Romy's eyes, which had grown wider and wider, now began to fill with mirth and she listened even more avidly and more shamelessly than before.

'I wonder now that she's appeared on the scene if Quila will change his allegiance.'

'I doubt it. Quila goes for quality.'

'Well, hasn't she got quality?'

'*And* quantity—if you know what I mean.' And there followed a guffaw of laughter.

The other man swore. 'If there's one thing that gets my goat, it's a know-all.'

'What gets your goat is the fact that I'm right most of the time and you know it. And I happen to be right this time as well. We were discussing the subject the other night when you weren't around. He doesn't go for flat-chested women.'

'Is she flat-chested?'

'Aren't all models? No meat on them anywhere.'

'She doesn't look exactly flat-chested.'

'When they say that photos don't lie, boyo, *that's* a lie. And something else he said, he doesn't go for females with, quote, bird-size brains, outsized egos and wall-to-wall teeth, unquote.'

At this, Romy almost choked and had to clamp a hand swiftly across her mouth to prevent her incredulity and humour from escaping in an audible mixture of giggles and outright laughter. A full five minutes elapsed before she felt sufficiently composed to confront the occupants of the men's quarters and in particular the two unknown conversationalists who were now, she guessed, eating and in relative silence.

By that time her amusement had dissipated somewhat and a mild indignation had begun to swell up in its place. Wall-to-wall teeth indeed! She straightened from her leaning position against the wall of the dwelling, mentally braced herself, and proceeded around to the main entrance.

She wasn't surprised to be told that Quila hadn't as yet turned up for breakfast, because if he had been present she doubted that their names would have been linked or that either of them would have been the targets for such frank discussion.

She was invited in to wait for him, and as she entered the men's residence she felt her customary self-assurance, which had always been a stable and ever faithful companion, waver precariously. The cause was not due to the crude yet clean and serviceable living quarters, nor to the awed quality of the sudden rather ringing silence which had descended upon the men at her entrance, but instead to the sight of the innumerable pictures which were pinned, tacked and taped at varying angles on both the walls and the ceiling—and all were of herself! They weren't very recent ones, and in fact must have been put up by the men who had occupied the quarters before these men. Probably local labourers her father had hired who knew her or of her, and probably many of them by the shearers who had known her long before she had won the contest that was to change her life.

It was a long time since she had experienced an

embarrassment quite like this. And there was no
escaping it, for no matter where or how often she
averted her gaze, there to confront her was another
array of pictures, faded and some not so faded, black
and white and some in colour, both good shots and
bad shots, in all modes of dress and in all situations,
from a bikini in a beach setting, and shorts and top in
a sports setting, to the most seductive evening gown in
a romantic evening setting.

Her embarrassment must have transferred itself to
the men present, for the feet of the older ones began to
shuffle and the faces of the younger ones had taken on
a slight pinkish hue. Romy sat down on the rather
rickety wooden chair that had been fetched for her,
smiled awkwardly and hoped fervently that Quila
wouldn't be long in coming.

He wasn't. And the moment he came through the
door in faded cords and a plaid shirt, she was on her
feet. She could tell that he sensed immediately the difference in the atmosphere and when his eyes fell on
her she saw the inevitable controlling and tightening
of his expression. His eyes narrowed. 'What are you
doing here?'

Hardly an opening one could describe as being filled
with promise! Romy tilted her chin, slightly chagrined
by the manner he had adopted with her in front of
these men. 'I'd like to speak to you. Perhaps we could
go outside.'

His eyes seemed to narrow still further. 'You're on
my territory now, Miss Palliser. If you want something
from me, you ask me—politely.'

Taken aback, Romy could do or say nothing for a
moment or two. Then, reacting swiftly and with the
aplomb for which she had worked so hard and long to
acquire and which she was determined this time to

keep at her disposal at all costs, she graciously inclined her head. 'May I please speak to you alone? I won't take up too much of your time.'

He stood back and allowed her to proceed through the door before him. She intended that they should walk until she was quite certain that the men were out of earshot; however, Quila paused not far from the verandah steps and she knew instinctively that he intended to go no farther.

She came straight to the point. 'I'd like to go on a round of the farm.'

He nodded, slipping his hands into the back pockets of his cords. 'Just let me know when and I'll see to it that the keys to the Land Rover are left with Cook.'

'No, I don't mean by Land Rover. I want to go with you on horseback.'

He shrugged. 'That's fine by me. I'll get one of the lads to saddle you a horse. You can go with him.'

He was being deliberately obtuse and she knew it. He was also making no effort to lower his voice, so she abandoned her attempts to keep their conversation private. 'I don't want to go with one of the lads. I want to go with you. When do you think you can manage it?'

The line of his mouth became even straighter and, seeing it, Romy thought absently what a shame it was, because he was spoiling what could otherwise be a very attractive mouth and perhaps one of his better features. 'Will tomorrow morning be convenient?'

'Tomorrow morning will be fine. What time?'

'After breakfast—about seven-thirty.'

'Thank you.' She hesitated before turning away and looked up at him, and made a mistake by asking in a more modulated tone: 'Exactly what is it about me you find so—abhorrent?'

Quila lifted his gaze from the scuffed earth and met her quizzical one, then raised his head and said without haste or applied emphasis: 'I dislike organising, dictatorial, over-confident women in all circumstances, but more especially when they begin interfering in areas they know nothing whatsoever about. If you do find it necessary to come tomorrow—wear a bra.' Turning on his heel, he left her staring after him, dumbfounded.

There was no doubt whatsoever that the ears that had listened as avidly to their conversation as hers had earlier to another conversation had indeed heard that last spiel and most definitely Quila's parting shot.

She turned, more slowly than he had, and started back towards the homestead, walking with the fluidity of grace that had been taught and practised relentlessly until it had become so ingrained that it was in ever-widening degrees automatically applied to all her movements.

If it had been his intention to embarrass her, he hadn't succeeded. But she was no longer as light-hearted as she had been when she had first set out Instead his attitude had rendered her sober and thoughtful. He considered her stuck-up, she realised, too self-possessed and overbearing. Was that really how she appeared to people? Well, she refused to accept that she was stuck-up. Perhaps she was extremely self-confident and had come to be so by having been made totally aware over the years, and accept without quibbling, that she was liked by most people with whom she came into contact, and to be sought after by men was usually the outcome of each introduction.

But not so in Quila's case. Rather the very opposite. And because she was not used to being shunned by men, she was equally unused to dealing with it or coping with unpleasantness. She had never had any need for caustic repartee and so had seen no reason to build up one. It was no wonder she was at a loss.

By the time she had reached the homestead, she was both hot and irritable. And realising that she had allowed him to get to her soured her temper still further.

True to his word, Quila sent Leon down to lend his assistance in tidying the garden and restoring the tennis court and orchard to their respective original states. Leon's presence did much to lighten Romy's mood that day, for she found him very congenial company. He was shy and courteous but at the same time equipped with humour and an eagerness to work, traits which Romy found extremely pleasing. The fact that he was slightly in awe of her and, as a consequence, shyer than he might otherwise have been, didn't particularly worry her. It wouldn't take long to put him at his ease, and then she was sure he would be most acceptable company.

CHAPTER FIVE

THE following morning dawned bright and sunny, and
Romy dressed accordingly in a pair of old tan-coloured
jodhpurs which she found amongst the few clothes that
were still hanging in her wardrobe and not either
thrown or given away. To match, she donned a cream
long-sleeved cotton blouse which she was reluctant to
wear on such a venture but was compelled to since she
owned nothing more suitable. At least with this blouse
she could pull down the loosely rolled up sleeves to
cover her arms in the event of the sun's rays becoming
too fierce. With a wide-brimmed hat on her head, and
sunglasses, sweater, riding gloves and a packed lunch
in a small serviceable knapsack, she set off to the
stables.

Quila was ready and waiting for her with two saddled
horses, a gelding, Logos, and a mare, Tess, tied up at
the corral, looking fresh and frisky and more than ready
for their day's outing. Quila spared her but a cursory
glance and a few words of greeting before mounting
the gelding and taking advantage of his head start by
giving the horse its lead.

Unperturbed, Romy swung herself up on to the mare
and soon caught up with the horse in front. She didn't
draw up alongside him but chose to remain behind so
that she wouldn't have to encounter Quila's dour
countenance at every turn. She wanted to enjoy this,
her first tour of the farm in five years, and she fully
intended to. Already her heart was soaring at the
beauty which surrounded her, the smells exuded by

both the sun warmed earth and the animals alike.

Viewed from a distance, the hills resembled mounds of verdant velvet with overtones of blue, and the blades of grass nearer at hand bowed away from them and rippled and shone like silk in the sunny sea breeze. Blue grass, she thought suddenly. Was it that elusive bluish hue she fancied she could detect which gave rise to the term? Perhaps it wasn't as nonsensical as one would suppose.

As they rode, Romy paused every so often to glance over her shoulder at the homestead and its picturesque environs, and beyond at the sheltered bay which eventually widened out to meet with the vast ocean. Before her, the country was constantly varying, its gently undulating slopes giving way to rugged hill country, only to soften once more and become decidedly easier to traverse.

After an hour of their journeying separately, and consequently in silence, Quila stopped some distance ahead of her and by the time she had closed the gap between them he had dismounted and was striding across the nearby paddock to where one of the farmhands was on his knees beside the recumbent form of a sheep.

Romy also dismounted, slowly and carefully, because it had been a long time since she had sat astride a horse for more than an hour at one stretch, tied the reins to the fence, climbed over and crossed to where the two men were busy inspecting the sheep.

'Goddamn it, I think we're going to lose her!' the man was exclaiming to Quila.

'Her first?'

'Yeah. And this will be the third ewe this week. The lamb needs to be turned around but my hands are too damn big, and yours,' he said, glancing at Quila's hands, 'are no smaller.'

'Better get it done, then, we don't want to lose the lamb as well.'

'Perhaps I can help,' Romy piped up. 'My hands are considerably smaller than either of yours.'

For the first time the two men acknowledged her presence and the young shepherd looked questioningly from Romy to Quila. 'Rod, this is Miss Palliser, Matt Palliser's daughter.'

Rod gave her an answering smile and gestured in a way that conveyed to her that his hands were in no condition to make contact with hers.

'May I try?' she directed her question at Rod who, in surprise, merely looked to Quila for a suitable response.

'While we waste time trying to explain to you what to do, we could well lose both.'

This Romy ignored. Her eyes roved over Rod's equipment and catching sight of the antiseptic oil he had used, she went down on her haunches beside the labouring ewe, smeared the oil over her hands and up to the elbow of her right arm and set to work. Once she had turned the lamb, she positioned its head and brought out its two front hooves. Within seconds the lamb was lying, steaming a little and mewing weakly, on the grass before her. Romy gazed at it, delighted. Gently she picked it up and brought it around within touching distance of its mother's nose. 'There you are, girl, your very first lamb!' The ewe brought its head forward, gave her offspring one feeble lick and promptly fell back exhausted, seeming to possess no inclination to rally. 'She'll need some penicillin,' she said, looking up at Rod, who was in turn staring at her with admiration written all over his face.

'Boy, we sure could have done with you around this week! Couldn't we, Quila?'

'I really don't know how we managed without her all this time,' drawled Quila, and set off back across to the paddock to where the mounts were tethered.

Romy stared after him, flabbergasted. 'Well, if he isn't the absolute limit!' she thought, absently accepting the cloth Rod was offering her to clean her hands. 'I'll wash them in the trough, thanks, Rod.'

'Thank *you*. I hope you'll be sticking around, Miss Palliser.'

'Oh, I will be,' she assured him, and was gratified to some extent by the knowledge that by the time this story was spread around, she would have gone up in the estimation of the men if not Quila Morgan.

Once they had started off again, it didn't take Romy long to realise that Quila was no longer keeping to the track and that he was leading her over some of the most rugged terrain of the farm. Up over steep hillsides and down into deep, sharply plunging bush-clad gullies. Romy made no protest. She couldn't even if she had a mind to, for she needed to allot her total concentration and energy to the controlling of her mount. The task absorbed her and, no doubt contrary to Quila's intended objective, she was enjoying the challenge despite the fact that at times she was scared witless, and all the time she was hot, parched, pitched and jolted until she was convinced that every bone in her body must be dislocated. As for tomorrow, she'd be in so much pain that she'd want to physically administer the same torture on that surly brute ahead of her—but it didn't do to think about tomorrow. If she did she might just be tempted to call it quits, and her surrender was exactly what Quila was working towards. She would *never* give him the satisfaction!

All of a sudden the weather changed. The sun disappeared, the temperature dropped sharply and the clouds that had gathered thickened, changed from a beautiful air-force blue to a less appealing shade of charcoal grey and wasted no time in emptying their heavy burden on the thirsty earth. Within seconds, Romy was drenched to the skin and shivering with cold. Not so Quila, however, who hadn't been as pre-occupied as she with his mount and had donned an oilskin which he seemed to have conjured up from out of nowhere. All she had with her was a sweater which she hastily pulled on when Quila brought them on to more level ground. The sweater, of course, was soaked in seconds, but at least she was a little warmer and could relax and enjoy nature's sudden change of mood. She took off her hat and sunglasses and lifted her face, revelling in the feel of the rain beating on her skin and perspiring scalp.

When she opened her eyes it was just in time to catch Quila looking back at her over his shoulder and below the wide brim of his hat.

It wasn't the first time during this cross-country ordeal that he had looked back at her as if he was wait-ing expectantly to see signs from her indicating her desire to turn back. He'd wait a long time, she thought, curbing an impulse to poke out her tongue. It was teeming, the earth and her mount were steaming, she was drenched, and she was loving every moment of it. Other than the heavy patter of rain on the already sodden soil, there was no sound. No screeching or honking of traffic, no pushing and shoving of crowds, no stench of putrid odours and exhaust fumes. All was beautiful and clean and smelled simply wonderful. It was delicious! And so exultant was she that she laughed out loud.

As quickly as it began, the rain ceased. The sun re-appeared and shone down almost as warmly as before.

'Hey!' Romy shouted to Quila, who heeded her call, reined in and turned around.

'I'm starving. Do you think we could stop some place and eat?'

'Fancy a climb up Three Kings?' he called back, inclining his head towards the nearby three peaked hill. 'You've been away so long you've probably forgotten the view.'

Romy hadn't forgotten the view—nor the stupendous effort that was required in order to avail oneself of it. It was the highest point of the farm and she had climbed it many times when she was younger and fitter, and even then she had suffered the following day. In her mind she called Quila a few choice names before sliding down from her horse and beginning the slippery hike to the summit of Three Kings.

Upon her arrival at the top she was hot, breathless and exhausted, and made only a halfhearted attempt to conceal the fact before collapsing flat on her back on the wet grass to stare up at the blue cloud-dotted sky and watch it revolve around and around.

'You'd better use this,' said Quila briefly, withdrawing an oilskin sheet from his knapsack and spreading it on the ground.

Slowly Romy sat up, hoisted herself to her feet and pulled her sweater up over her head. She hung it over the nearby fence to dry and Quila did the same with his oilskin coat.

Once she had taken several long swigs at her flask of apple juice and water, she felt almost reborn. 'Like a sandwich?' she asked, dropping to her knees on the oilskin. When Quila told her that he had brought along his own food, she began to tuck in, grinning to herself as she tried in vain to be ladylike in her attempts to eat the doorstep sandwiches she had made and not wolf them down as the extent of her hunger seemed to demand.

Several times she had to change her position, and she grinned again when she tried to imagine the kind of wreck she would represent tomorrow.

Quila, seeing her grinning periodically, spoke, sounding annoyed. 'You seem inordinately happy.'

'I am,' she told him, her face full of laughter. 'Everything is so lovely, so clean and smells so good. I'm so glad to be back.'

'For how long?'

'For a long time. Sorry to disappoint you.' She knelt up, wiped her hands on the thighs of her jodhpurs and then raised them to the wet lank ponytail which hung down her back. She pulled the elastic from her hair and shook it free, then ran her fingers through it to loosen it and allow the sun to dry it. The upper layers were already quite dry and sprang into the kind of untamed curls and waves that had not been brought under subjection by a brush and blowdryer. The short strands curled about her forehead and framed the fine pure lines of her face. Her actions had been totally unpremeditated and unselfconscious, and when she glanced at Quila again she was startled to discover that his eyes were resting on the slender curves of her body. When they lifted to meet hers, she sensed no awkwardness and could detect no embarrassment. He appeared unabashed and as usual his expression was quite fathomless.

'Didn't I tell you to wear a bra?'

Romy looked down at herself and found that the front of her shirt was still wet and had moulded itself to her body. Although she coloured slightly, she remained unflustered. She pulled at the material. 'You did. And I am.'

'Then I suggest you oblige me further and come up with something a little more substantial. You're no longer keeping company with the blasé and pleasure-weary sophisticates of New York, as I'm sure you're well aware. I don't want to be placed in a position where I have to remind you another time.'

At a complete loss, Romy silently sprang to her feet and strode away from him, walking as far as she could along the top of the hill and so putting as much distance between them as possible.

Once again she had, without difficulty, managed to earn Quila's disapproval and another lash from his scathing tongue. By nature she was a sunny, easy-going person, and it took immense provocation before she succumbed to anger. And right now she was more perplexed than angry. If only she could understand what it was about her that he found so unendurable, so—distasteful! One thing was for sure, she wouldn't go on indefinitely accepting this kind of treatment. To a certain extent he had been right about her mode of dress and she acceded his point, but all the same, there was no call for him to denigrate her the way he was doing. It wasn't as if she hadn't heeded and tried to concur with his wishes. At this rate the time would no doubt come, she suspected, when his attitude would cease to puzzle her and begin to annoy her intensely.

Leaning against a fence post, she gazed out across the spring-green hills and valleys over which they had come and to the pale dot which was the homestead standing amidst the trees and beyond to where the horizon of the blue Pacific met up with the paler blue sky. By the time she had taken in her fill of the view and had returned to the spot where they had eaten, she found Quila lying back asleep, one arm pillowing his head while the other lay slackly across his middle.

'Good!' she exclaimed to herself, and dropped to her
knees once more, sitting back on her ankles and reaching for the orange she had only partly consumed. 'I
wouldn't mind betting you too won't escape from a
few aches and pains tomorrow!'

Even asleep he gave nothing away, she thought,
taking the opportunity to study his face without fear of
detection. A quiet set expressionless face hiding—what
kind of man? All she could be sure of was that his
tolerance of her was practically non-existent. Perhaps
he withheld forgiveness from anyone whom he considered owned a character weaker or more flawed than
his own. But she couldn't be sure. She couldn't judge,
because she had nothing to go on. Not that the fact
that he knew nothing first-hand about her prevented
him from prejudging her, it seemed.

She went on to wonder whether he could be described as handsome, or even good-looking. Taken one
by one, his features were attractive enough, but overall
she supposed that conventionally speaking they would
have to be called regular, which could categorise him
as 'plain'. But then perhaps the somewhat pugnacious
line of his jaw and the grooves on either side of his
mouth saved him from being totally nondescript. His
skin, she thought, was his best feature, matt and
smooth with a slight sheen, and tanned, though not
from exposure to a great deal of sunshine, for winter
had only just passed, but due to long periods spent
outdoors living in the face of all kinds of weather.

She turned her back on him, assumed a cross-legged
position and tackled the remainder of her orange.
Licking the last of the juice from her fingers and
around her mouth, she turned once more to glance at
Quila, only to discover that he was no longer asleep.

Propped up on one elbow, he was very much awake and subjecting her to as close a scrutiny as she had subjected him, only there was a difference in his regard as it rested sombrely on her hair, now dry, streaked with lighter colour and tossed into glorious disarray by her fingers and the mild but persistent breeze. It came to her instinctively that he was seeing her as she had been on her knees in her wet clinging blouse, with her arms upraised and her fingers threading through her hair. As their eyes met her senses stirred and she was suffused by an inner heat.

She refused to look away, wanting suddenly, almost urgently, to know exactly what he was thinking, what he was feeling and if, despite his apparent self-professed dislike of her and her looks, he could actually feel some stirrings of desire for her. The power she had had over some of the men of her acquaintance had never meant anything to her, but nugatory and valueless though she considered the talent to be, it had been one of which she could always be sure. No longer, it seemed. With other men she had intuitively known, but with Quila she was unable to decide.

And what threatened to make the entire situation intolerable was the suspicion that if the upheaval of her senses was anything to go by, she could well find herself in a situation of reversed circumstances wherein he could quite likely be the possessor of the power ... Abruptly, she caught herself and brought a swift end to the runaway nature of her thoughts. This really was insane! Dallying no further, she rose with litheness to her feet and crossed to where her sweater was draped over the fence and, sensing that her every movement was being openly observed, kept her back to him as she tied her sweater about her shoulders and once more caught her hair back into a ponytail.

Without obvious haste, she gathered together her scattered belongings and food scraps, thrust them into her knapsack and began the descent down Three Kings to where their mounts were grazing.

By the time they arrived back at the stables, Romy was suffering from what was only a foretaste of the pain she knew she was going to have to endure the next day. Of course Quila would be more than qualified to make a pretty accurate assumption of how she was feeling, but not wanting to provide him with the actual visual evidence, she dismounted as nimbly as her protesting body would allow. Then, to her dismay, he indicated that he expected her to unsaddle and groom her mount, just as he was doing. Gritting her teeth, she silently followed his example, and by the time she was finished she was bathed in perspiration and dizzy from over-exertion.

She knew that Quila had deliberately taken her on a wild goose chase across the farm and in so doing daring her to beg off, to decline to climb Three Kings and refuse to groom her horse, but as she walked beside him in silence around the corrals towards the men's quarters, she had neither the inclination nor the energy for anger or resentment. Besides, she had to admit she had thoroughly enjoyed the initial stages of the expedition if not so much the later ones, and it had been only her discomfort that had denied her that enjoyment.

Catching a whiff of herself, she wrinkled her nose. She was certainly no advertisement for deodorant or French perfume at that moment! And neither was Quila. But funnily enough, she didn't consider the mingling odours of horse and fresh sweat that emanated from him to be offensive. In fact it was a welcome change from the world she had just come from, where the atmosphere seemed permanently thick with cloying perfume and aftershave and redolent of smoke from numerous brands of tobacco, and where men were suave and sophisticated, bedecked in jewellery and always sweetly smelling. The smell now in her nostrils reminded her of when she was younger, riding and working alongside her father and all at once her spirits were uplifted. Forgetting her aches and pains, she cast Quila a sidelong look and as he turned his head slightly and caught it, she gave him a tentative smile, but didn't continue to watch to see if it was returned, certain it wouldn't be.

'Thank you for giving up your day to take me on an escorted tour,' she said. 'I enjoyed it.'

'You're the boss's daughter. Did I have a choice?'

'I suppose not, but you'll have your revenge tomorrow. I think you saw to that.' She felt him shoot her a sideways glance, but she kept her gaze fixed firmly on the view ahead of her.

'I wanted to make sure that you saw all that you wanted to see, that's all. I hope your mind's been set at rest as regards your opinion of my capabilities when it comes to farming and the managing of Summerhaze.'

Was he expecting a pat on the back from her? Then he'd wait an eternity, especially when he had made it abundantly clear on several occasions that she could expect no commendation from him. 'Like you, I guess I'm pretty reluctant when it comes to handing out bouquets,' she replied. 'Let's just say that my opinion of you probably just about matches your opinion of me. As for your farming capabilities, I wouldn't say I was questioning them exactly. I only wanted to see for myself what kind of state the farm is in. A lot has happened since I've been away.'

'Yes, on that at least we can agree,' he replied, on

such a grim and rather enigmatic note that Romy wanted to throw him a quick searching glance, but she managed in time to restrain the urge, acknowledging that it would have proved fruitless.

For the two to three days that followed, Romy was unable to work alongside Leon and help clear the creeper, weeds and various grasses which choked the high wire fence surrounding the tennis court. However, far from being rendered totally inactive, she spent a great deal of her time skinning and bottling the dark red end-of-season tamarillos which she and Leon had salvaged from the orchard preceding her tour of the farm. Many of the overripe ones she made into jam and gave several jars of both jam and fruit to Leon to take up with him to the cook.

By the third day, she was beginning to feel more like her normal self. The humour her father had found in her incapacity began to dwindle, and the house reeked less of liniment and there were fewer exclamations accompanying her more sudden movements.

She had outlined to Leon her plan to invite a group of I.H.C. children over from Wellington to spend the day on the farm, and he immediately championed her idea and volunteered his help if it was required. So during her recuperating period, Romy spent an entire afternoon making the necessary phone calls and planning a menu and a day of games and activities which she knew from past experience the children would enjoy to the fullest extent.

The same afternoon she wrote to the manager of a prominent Wellington department store who, having learned from some source of her arrival back in New Zealand, had written and invited her to take part in their summer fashion parades to be held that year in one of the city's foremost hotels. She had mulled over her decision for two days before finally replying in the affirmative. Why not? she thought. For not only would it give her a break away and a time to think outside of the environment she loved and which tended to colour her thoughts and so would inevitably influence the decisions she might have to make with regards to her future, but it would also bring her back into the kind of life style she had told herself she had given up for good. Perhaps another scant taste of the limelight and world of glamour and fashion would help confirm that decision and convince her that her desire to lead such a life had indeed gone and for good.

The fashion parades were to run for three days and were scheduled for the middle of November, four weeks away, which meant that the children's picnic could be fitted in ideally between now and then.

The spring was proving extremely unpredictable, she thought, as she sat at the desk in the room her father had turned into and referred to as the library, staring out at the rain beating down through the trees and rolling off the waxy surfaces of the young bright green leaves. The famous hot east coast sunshine had disappeared the previous afternoon and hadn't even so much as peeped through the thick grey mass of formless clouds since. It was even difficult to believe that only a few short days before she had been out riding beneath a sun that had scorched the earth and borne down on her so relentlessly that she had felt, among other things, like a blob of melted butter. Now, seated at the large kauri desk, surrounded by countless shelves of books, trophies, ribbons and other mementoes and looked down upon by a massive wapiti stag head and a large aerial photograph of Summerhaze itself, she felt that even if she were to sit on top of it she still wouldn't be close enough to the two-bar electric heater. She sighed and returned to her task of letter writing, hoping for the children's sake that the day she had chosen for their picnic would be fine and warm.

Her wish was granted. In fact, Romy was sure that even a Monday in the middle of summer couldn't possibly have been hotter than this Monday promised to be. As for Leon, any doubts she might have entertained about his usefulness and ability to respond swiftly to the children's needs and demands were dispelled so quickly, she could have buckled beneath the tide of relief.

The food she and her mother had so painstakingly prepared the day before was set up outside on the paper-covered trestles Leon had helped erect beneath the trees on the front lawn. The rules to the games which Romy had spent weeks groping for from the recesses of her mind were explained quickly to Leon and to the women who had accompanied the group, and the twenty children threw themselves into each new venture with gleeful abandon. The noise and hilarity was at such a pitch, Nina gave voice to her misgivings that the birds, so used to the quiet peaceful environs of Summerhaze, would flee and never return. And although she had apparently forgotten the vociferous manifestations of the children's enjoyment on previous occasions, Romy hadn't, and she was privately revelling in the chaotic conditions and the opportunity to let her hair down and shout and laugh and race and tumble with the children. She was reluctant to call a halt to such antics in order to follow the more sedate pursuit, but one she knew instinctively the children loved best, of becoming acquainted with the animals.

Leon was an absolute angel, she kept telling herself as she watched the gentle way in which he brought the children and the animals together, ensuring that each child got a ride on the pony which he had managed to persuade Quila to relinquish into his keeping for the day and for this purpose—the way, too, that he patiently demonstrated how the children were to hold the young, late season lambs and feed the calves and nurse the fluffy, newly hatched chicks.

Since it had turned out to be such a fine day, a swim had also been planned, but Margery Lorne, the woman in charge of the group, decided in the end to relinquish this idea, expressing her opinion that the children had already had any amount of excitement for one day. To this Romy conceded, so instead they settled on finishing off the day with a cold drink and cookies consumed before a hastily improvised puppet show.

'Wow!' groaned Leon, staring about him after the bus had departed, rubbing his hands over his ears. 'My ears are ringing with the silence!'

Romy laughed. 'And mine. I only hope Mum's not right and that those birds that took flight actually do come back.' She turned to him and touched his arm lightly, briefly, her green eyes turned almost silver by the brightness of the sunny afternoon. 'How can I thank you enough for all your help this afternoon? What on earth would I have done without you?'

The youth's smooth tanned skin reddened a little and he looked hastily away from her. 'Oh, I didn't do anything,' he disclaimed awkwardly.

'You most certainly did. If it hadn't been for you I wouldn't have known if I were on my head or my heels. I wonder if Mum is right and that they actually were more boisterous this time than they were five years ago.' She laughed, then wiped the back of her wrist over her forehead and exclaimed: 'Goodness, it's so *hot*! What do you say we have that swim we were going to have with the kids?'

Leon's eyes widened and lit up for an instant before the anticipation died. 'But we have all this to clear up.'

'Oh, that can wait. Have you got your swimsuit? Good. But instead of the bay, let's saddle some horses and ride out to the river—I bet you haven't been there yet?'

'No, I haven't . . .'

'Then that's settled. I know a swimming hole there surrounded by willows and gum trees, and the water— if my memory serves me correctly—is like silk. Come with me first and I'll let Mum know where we're off to.'

Within twenty minutes they were astride their mounts and heading in the direction of the hills, the more distant ones appearing dark and bruised with the higher surfaces caught by sunlight glowing an almost phospherescent green, while the hollows and crevices took on hues of blue and purple and their gently moulded peaks were lost to sight beneath swirls of thick ominous cloud.

They stopped their mounts close to the waterhole Romy had last swum in six years before. She and Julie had often gone swimming here with their cousins, but that had been during their early to mid-teens. She and Julie hadn't done anything together for a long time now, and they weren't likely to in the future either, it seemed.

Together, she and Leon dismounted and tethered the horses in the shade while they went to inspect the waterhole. Would it be as she remembered it? Rather apprehensively, Romy made her way through the trees which consisted of more varieties than simply willows and gums, but it had been these two kinds which had figured predominantly in her memory. There was no beaten track through the trees as there had been once. The only living creatures now to wander beneath the trees and disturb the grass during these latter years were four-legged, woolly-coated ones. What a shame! Such a waste, she thought, coming to the rocky clearing and gazing with delight at the deep gently swirling waters dappled by the late afternoon sunlight that filtered through the trees.

'Last one in,' Romy shouted, pulling off her T-shirt, 'has to groom *both* horses!' With a quick flick of her wrists, her hair was knotted and her hands descended to the zip of her jeans.

But the thundering of fast approaching horse's hooves was a sound that stilled the movements of both of them. They glanced at each other, puzzlement in their eyes, before looking expectantly towards the clearing through which they themselves had walked.

To Romy's utter amazement, Quila himself appeared, and she couldn't have been more astounded had she actually seen Leon conjure him up out of a hat.

Before she could recover herself to say anything at all, Quila spoke in a sharp undertone to Leon: 'On your horse and back to the quarters!'

'What?' was all Romy could manage, still dumbstruck.

But Quila didn't look at her, or acknowledge her presence. She might not have even existed, much less spoken.

'You heard me,' he said quietly to Leon, and this time Leon didn't look towards her as if for assistance, a word in his favour. He silently picked up his hat and shirt from where he had flung them and pulled on his discarded shoes.

'Now just a minute, Quila!' Romy protested strongly. 'We were just about to take a swim.'

Quila looked at her then and it took all her will power not to recoil visibly from the cold, undisguised contempt in the eyes that swung to meet hers. 'Over your actions, I hold no sway,' he said, reining in on his frisky mount, 'but Leon knows what's expected of him and while working here, he does as I say.'

'But surely he's entitled to some free time,' argued Romy, trying to sound reasonable. 'We've finished for the day.'

'You might finish for the day at four o'clock. Leon doesn't. If you knock off at four, he carries on or he returns to the men to see if anything needs to be done.'

'Look, I do think you're being just a little unfair. He spent a lot of his day off yesterday helping me prepare for today. And he worked through his lunch break today.'

'That was his choice.' He jerked his head at Leon, indicating that he should go, mount up and head back to the quarters.

When the youth had disappeared without argument through the trees, Quila once more gave Romy the benefit of his icy stare. 'I've only one thing to say to you,' he said. 'Leave the youngster alone.'

Once again, Romy was completely flummoxed. 'What on earth are you talking about?'

And before she had gathered her wits, he had dismounted and was standing before her, controlling his restless horse by the reins without taking his eyes off her for an instant. 'You know what I mean,' he said in a low but forceful tone. 'Exactly what I say. He's only a boy, young and impressionable, with no experience of the world, and especially no experience of women like you.'

'Women like me?' Romy echoed. She didn't know whether she was affronted or not. She didn't know what she was or what it was she should be—only that he had succeeded in totally disconcerting her by this quite unexpected attack. 'You make it sound like a disease—women like me,' she rolled the phrase around on her tongue, suddenly deciding to be amused, for the time being at least, and try to sort out a more appropriate reaction later.

'Keep away from him. If you're looking for a diversion, choose someone closer to yourself in age and experience.'

'Oh?' She lifted an eyebrow at him and drew one cheek in between her teeth, still portraying amusement while something was telling her that by rights she should be angry—furiously angry. 'Someone like—you, for instance?'

His eyes swept her disparagingly, making her aware of the low but flattering cut of her bathing suit and simultaneously glad that she hadn't shed her jeans before he arrived on the scene. 'I doubt if even I could match you in the latter,' he said, and turned away and mounted his horse. 'You might be woman enough to excite a reciprocation from some men, but I guess I'm what you modern-day females term as a chauvinist. I favour the double standard and prefer a woman to be less experienced than I.'

Romy allowed him the final say and stood back as he swung his mount around, watching, her eyes squinting in the slanting sunlight, as he galloped off the way he had come.

Her amusement, if indeed that was what it had been,

had well and truly evaporated even before he was out of sight, and she was left feeling exasperated, indignant and even faintly depressed. She crossed over to a huge slab of rock that protruded out over the water and sat down upon it, drawing up her knees. All desire for a swim had been entirely vanquished. Goodness, what a boor he was! Mannerless, humourless and incredibly ignorant. Not a scrap like his sophisticated, charming, city-dwelling counterparts. But then wasn't that the facet about him she had been considering his most attractive attribute, possibly his only redeeming feature? She sighed. Stupid, stupid man! As if she would for a minute entertain the notion of seducing a sweet, innocent, fresh-faced boy like Leon. The mere thought of it appalled her, so how could Quila possibly believe her to be capable of such an action?

Then, for the first time, it occurred to her just how low his opinion of her must be. Her eyes widened at the insight and she pressed the fingers of one hand against her lips. What on earth *had* she done to give him grounds on which to draw such conclusions about her?

Was it really possible—could it be true that she was as trite and shallow as he so obviously seemed to think her? Beautiful but empty. To suspect such a thing had never entered her head. Now that it had, she was made afraid—horribly afraid that it was he who was actually seeing her as she really was.

Always she had been confident and self-assured with men, all of whom had been ready to fall at her feet if she so wished it of them. But she had cared for none of them in return. Not one. At the time, she couldn't have cared if none of them had ever yearned to kiss her, and never had she permitted any of them to venture beyond that point. To wonder at her unvarying response to every man she dated had never occurred to her, and without a qualm she had simply put their failure to elicit from her a more passionate response down to the fact that none of her suitors came bearing the old-fashioned designation of 'Mr Right.'

Now she was faced with the distinct possibility that she was the one at fault, the failure. Perhaps the truth was that she was just an attractive, untenanted frame and always had been, incapable of any depth or any genuine, lasting, heartrending emotion—inadequate!

No! She shot to her feet, her heart contracting with very real fright. No, she could never believe that, and she wouldn't waste another valuable second on this introspective investigation. What Quila thought of her, or why, simply wasn't important.

And because she knew herself to be quite alone, she stripped off down to the skin and took a long leisurely bathe, deliberately divesting her mind of all thoughts and concentrating instead on the calm, salubrious beauty of the late afternoon, the stillness, apart from the gently flowing and lapping of the water, and the quietness now that the birds were preparing for sleep.

Remarkably refreshed, she dried herself and dressed and in a new attitude of mind, she made her way back to where her mount, Tess, was standing, perfectly still, silhouetted against the setting sun, appearing to be dozing in its warmth.

CHAPTER SIX

As far as Romy was concerned, the break away from Summerhaze which her trip to Wellington provided couldn't have come at a more opportune time. While acknowledging the fact that if she had her way she would never leave Summerhaze again, she knew in her heart that a few days away from the tension evoked by her sister's sullen moods, quick flashes of temper and constant black looks would not only be a respite for her, but possibly for Julie as well. Surely this perpetual antipathy between them couldn't go on for ever? But what could she do about it, other than hope that Quila Morgan would make the most of her absence and continue to see as much of Julie as he must have done before her homecoming?

Even as the thought flashed through her mind, she was given a foretaste of the uneasiness which was to be left in its wake. She had had dealings with Quila subsequent to her original belief that any ambition he might possess to inherit Summerhaze through a union with Julie would be queered by Julie's own refusal to live out her life in a place she detested, and these encounters with Quila had disclosed to her that he was a man of determination. She could no longer envisage his being thwarted by anyone, not even a woman with whom he fell in love.

The opportunity to pursue this line of thought to some satisfactory or unsatisfactory conclusion didn't immediately arise, for Wednesday in Wellington passed in a whirl of the kind of activity she had become

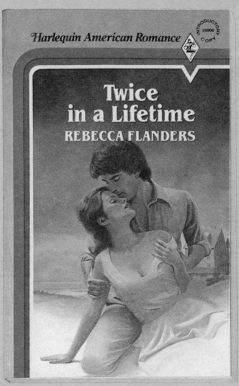

TWICE IN A LIFETIME

Rebecca Flanders

CHAPTER ONE

BARBARA sat in the crowded airport lounge, waiting for her flight to be called, and fingered the letter of invitation from her sister somewhat uncertainly. Barbara was twenty-six years old, self-sufficient, and mature, and she had been managing her own life since the first day she had left home for the independence of the state university. But, sitting alone amid the bustle and confusion of excited travelers, she felt somewhat like a lost and frightened child. She had felt that way a lot since Daniel had died.

She had been widowed a little over a year, and she knew her sister, via long-distance conferences with their mother, was worried about her. Perhaps with good cause, Barbara had to admit uneasily, for although most of the time Barbara managed to convince herself she was getting along just fine, there were still feelings of bitterness and periods of black depression she did not seem to be able to control. Of course it was a tragedy to be widowed so young, and everyone commiserated, everyone claimed to understand what she was going through. The real tragedy was that no one understood. No one could understand what it was to lose the one and only love of her life, not just a husband, but a lover and a friend... Most people would go their entire lives without ever finding what she and Daniel had shared, and to have their life together severed so abruptly and so cruelly was more than unfair, it was incomprehensible...

But Barbara wasn't meant to be alone for long. Follow her as she rediscovers the beauty of love. Read the rest of "Twice in a Lifetime" FREE.

so accustomed to over the preceding five years and there was no time to think about anything other than the job in hand. And she enjoyed every minute of it—the bright lights, appreciative audiences, fashion chatter, press, photographers and interviewers, hairdressers and the soft swirl of the new and ever-changing summer fabrics of the fashions she was selected to present. The day ended with a celebratory dinner from which she excused herself rather early, she had to admit, but she had worked hard and the excitement of the day's succession of events had left her quite enervated.

She had elected to stay in a hotel that was associated in no way with the events of that day, and the hubbub which promised to continue at the same pace for the following two days, and so, in compliance with her wishes, the parade organisers had booked her into an older type hotel in the centre of the city which possessed a more mellow character and atmosphere which she personally preferred.

Her room was a large one, with a high beamed ceiling and a floral-patterned wool carpet on the floor in which wine was featured as the principal colour. Deep wine-coloured curtains hung at the single window and fell all the way to the floor. On the double bed lay a thick lacy cream cover under which was a bedspread of pale rose taffeta. There was a central overhead light, but Romy preferred the soft muted glow shed by the two antique-fashioned lamps affixed to two of the cream-papered spaces in the predominantly panelled walls and situated several feet out from either side of a tall mirror that topped the dressing table.

Romy was enchanted with her room and didn't mind how much time she spent there. She had, and liked, the feeling that if she sat straight-backed on the side of her bed for long enough, an appropriately attired maid would knock at her door and come in, bearing a porcelain basin for her to wash in and a matching jug full of warm scented water with which to wash. Or, if she were to cross to her window and draw the curtains, she would see horse-drawn carriages travelling along dirt roads and men and women strolling arm in arm along elevated sidewalks, fabulously attired to suit the period of the mid-1800s. However, Romy didn't part the curtains, but retired instead to dream of the bygone era.

Thursday followed much the same pattern as Wednesday, and it was on this day that Romy knew with absolute certainty that she no longer wanted to continue to make her living this way. She had thoroughly enjoyed it while she had been able to accept her work without thinking, without analysing what she was doing and why, what she was doing with her life and for what reason she was living. But no longer could she blithely carry on living that kind of life. Her needs then, or at least those she had recognised, had been few and relatively undemanding. Now it seemed as though they had increased and had expanded and deepened, and yet were still apparently as nameless as before.

In a sober mood, she excused herself from joining the ebullient crowd at dinner and returned to the peace and quiet of her own hotel. Stepping into the foyer, she was about to utter a sigh of relief and drop into a nearby chair, when she caught sight of a dark-haired man who was of average height and build but whose very distinctive air and carriage banished completely all awareness of problems, lethargy and aching feet as though from that instant they had ceased to exist.

The man turned from the reception desk at that

moment and with key in hand strode towards the stairs. He disappeared around the curve in the stairs without having spotted her, and the return of her desire to drop down into the nearest chair was twice as strong as it had originally been. But she didn't dare succumb to it. Taking her key, she went directly to her room, kicked off her sandals, then with an unshod foot swung the door closed and fell back on to her bed with a sigh deeper than she had intended the first to have been.

What on earth was Quila Morgan doing here? Why wasn't he back on Summerhaze where he ought to be, earning the wages her father was paying him? And dating and falling in love with her sister? She halted her thoughts abruptly, for the latter thought was one which was becoming increasingly unpalatable and she had to own to experiencing a sense of relief at the realisation that Quila actually wasn't back at Summerhaze availing himself of the opportunity to reduce her sister to a state of acquiesence into which love might well have the power to tumble her. While she tried, she couldn't for the life of her bring herself to believe that Julie, or any woman for that matter, could have a similar effect on him. He appeared to be far too calm and in control of himself—so much so that she was having more and more difficulty in imagining him unbending sufficiently to fall in love with anyone. However, she now had to admit that she could understand how Julie could find him attractive. Dressed casually as he had been in pale slacks, an open-necked cream shirt which enhanced his tan, and a dark forest green jacket, he had made a very presentable picture indeed.

She yawned and stretched with the abandonment privacy granted her, and at that point in her musings she dozed off.

When she awoke again an hour later, she had totally

forgotten about Quila Morgan and his presence in the hotel. She showered and dressed for dinner and only became reacquainted with the rather disagreeable fact when she caught sight of him already seated in the dining-room. Seeing no point in delaying the inevitable, she told the dining-room hostess that she would join him and so made her way towards his table.

He looked up and saw her at the very moment that a group of three young men intercepted her as she was about to pass their table and asked her to join them. It was a situation she was well used to handling with both charm and poise. She obliged them by stopping at their table, but declined their invitation, and because she took a liking to the look of them and their jovial yet polite manner, as well as being aware that had they been on their own not one of them would have had the courage to broach her, she paused and chatted to them for several minutes before carrying on to Quila's table.

'Good evening. Do you mind if I join you?' As usual, she received no smile in response to her own and she wondered if the reluctance with which he rose and drew out a chair for her was as blatantly obvious to any of the other diners present as it was to her. For she was sure that the eyes of the majority of the diners were on them, since she had already claimed a certain amount of attention. She was looking exceptionally elegant in a simply designed, grape-coloured dress, with her hair coiled up into an attractive loose style and her face made up sparingly, though expertly, with her accomplished hand having employed all the tricks she had learned over the years. But for all the response she had drawn from Quila Morgan, she might just as well have been wearing a sack tied in the middle.

With a slight philosophical shrug she sat down, quickly ran her eye over the menu, then put it aside.

'Well, I suppose the obvious opening is: "What a surprise. I never expected to see you here."'

'Likewise.'

'When did you arrive?'

'Monday.'

'Holiday?'

'Business.'

The waiter came and Romy gave him her order, and after he had gone, she sat back in her chair and stared intently at Quila who didn't, it seemed, intend to allow her unwelcome intrusion to spoil his appetite. She tried again: 'When do you return to Summerhaze?'

'Depends. Don't worry,' sardonically, 'I'm not playing truant.'

For the first time she felt a genuine spark of anger against this man, an urge to do or say something that would succeed in shaking him out of the complacency that told how sure of himself he was when it came to the opinions he had formed about her. Her palm itched to strike that twist from his lips which he donned especially for her benefit and rip aside that expressionlessness that cloaked his features whenever she was around. How she was beginning to detest that—that most of all.

'What is it, Quila?' she asked with unconcealed curiosity. 'What have I done to make you dislike me so?'

He looked at her and appeared unmoved by her question. 'Surely,' he glanced past her, his gaze coming to rest significantly on the three young men who had stopped her and asked her to join them, 'the admiration of three men must more than make up for the lack of it in one. Three out of four isn't a bad average.'

'I didn't mention admiration,' Romy pointed out, adopting a tone of dryness. 'Knowing you don't admire me is neither here nor there. Dislike is something else altogether. I had the feeling you disliked me before you'd even met me.'

'I don't dislike you,' he denied, finishing his meal and resting his table napkin down on the table beside his plate. He looked directly at her. 'I just find it difficult to tolerate a person who should want to indulge in such a mindless and frivolous occupation such as yours.'

'Modelling?'

'That is your occupation, isn't it?'

She inclined her head and smiled at the waiter as he placed her meal of grilled fish and salad before her. 'Don't you like to see a woman looking attractive and well groomed?' she asked, taking up her fork.

'It's what the occupation lends itself to that I object to.'

She looked at him, baffled.

'Debauchery,' he said baldly and with no hint of apology for his belief. 'Can you deny it?'

Romy gave his question some thought. Then: 'Not in all cases, but I most certainly can in my own. Do I look debauched?' she asked, trying to look artless, but a mischievous twinkle dancing in her eyes gave her away.

Quila put down his glass, now empty of beer, and replied: 'No. But you're still young and attractive. When looks fade, who knows? You, like many other women, may become desperate to recapture what's gone and go to any lengths to live again times that are over and done with.'

'Perhaps the secret is to know when to retire,' she shrugged.

'And you know that secret?'

'I've retired.'

His mask had become dislodged to make way for an

expression of sceptism. Well, she thought, it was a start. Aloud she said: 'I've been thinking about it for a number of months now. Today, I decided for sure. I came to Wellington for the express purpose of modelling for one of the department stores in town in their summer fashion parades which are being held at the James Cook. They started yesterday, were repeated today and will be repeated for the final time tomorrow. My last appearance,' she grinned wryly. 'I should have given up years ago, but then of course it's easy to say that now, because it's only now that I recognise the need and the time. You're right—there is debauchery and I saw it, but I had no part in it. I had no need to involve myself that way, because I was successful in my own right and would have been successful no matter what. And if I'd needed to resort to seeking string-pullers to get to the top, I would have bowed out. The pinnacle would never have been that important to me.' He still didn't believe her, she realised, but what did it matter? At least she had his attention. And wonder of wonders, he was interested!

'It was a plastic world full of plastic people, dissipated men and women with embryonic souls, very much alike in that they used each other, fed off one another, competed, vied, preyed until that time you mentioned came round and they were discarded like so many car wrecks in a wrecker's yard. But don't get me wrong, it wasn't all like that. I had a lot of wonderful experiences and right now I wouldn't trade one.'

Abruptly, Quila made to rise, but before he did so she felt compelled to at least try to wipe that look of wearied cynicism off his face. 'I *know* what I'm talking about. Exactly what is it that makes you consider you're such an authority?'

He stood up and pushed in his chair. 'A qualification

equal to your own, believe me,' he replied enig-
matically, and excusing himself, he strode away and
left her, and neither her professional training nor any
amount of self-admonition or pondering on his parting
remark could aid her in this instance. She felt con-
spicuous and quite frankly humiliated. Nevertheless,
she finished eating her dinner, striving to appear, outwardly at least, at ease and enjoying both her meal and
the pleasant piped repertoire of Mantovani's music.

She'd never get through to him, she thought. His
mind was firmly made up about her and the life she
led and had led, and she could try talking to him until
she was blue in the face and still she would make no
real impression. Bigoted was what he was—through
and through. This time when she passed the three
young men, still seated at their table, she accepted their
invitation to join them in the house bar for a drink and
took excessive pleasure in ignoring, totally, Quila's
presence there.

The following day, being Friday and the last day of
the parades, was especially hectic, and although it was
not in Romy's nature not to enjoy and make the best
of whatever she was doing, she still couldn't help
thinking longingly of Summerhaze and her imminent
return to its quiet and comparatively deserted surroundings, and she wondered to herself just how she
had managed to tolerate such fever-pitched action as
this for as long as she had.

The crowds which assembled that day, both before
and after the lunchtime parades, were considerably
larger than those of the previous two days, and it was
practically impossible for Romy, even if she had
wanted to, to single out any one face from the sea of
upturned faces belonging to the people pressing closely
around the catwalks. How then her eyes were drawn to

one male countenance, more tanned than those of the people in front of him, she couldn't understand. Magnetism, she joked to herself as she changed from one flimsy evening gown into another. And perhaps it had been, for when she stepped out on to the catwalk again she felt no pull to look on the direction of where he had been standing and she knew immediately that Quila Morgan had gone.

Curiously her spirits sank and although she tried, she seemed powerless to revive them. He had gone, something within her persisted in acknowledging. Gone—back to Summerhaze. Good heavens, she kept chiding herself, this was ridiculous! She should be relieved—rejoicing even—not feeling as though every light in Wellington had suddenly been snuffed out. And so she was, and to prove it she was going to stay in Wellington and spend the entire weekend relaxing and exploring at leisure.

At ten o'clock she withdrew from the merrymaking and celebrations which her jubilant colleagues of the past three days seemed to want to prolong indefinitely, and returned to her hotel, reminding herself of her resolve and drawing a synthetic kind of comfort from it.

On her way to her room, she decided to cut through the hotel lounge and purchase a bottle of ginger ale from the house bar. Sipping ginger ale had often worked in the past when her entire constitution had become indignant at the extensive bouts of tension and excitement, rich foods and excessive smoke inhalation it had been expected to absorb and contend with. On the whole, she was far too fatigued and strangely dispirited to take note of her surroundings and those who moved about in them, so it was quite by accident that she happened to see Quila sitting in one of the lounge's chairs, appearing to be deeply engrossed in a book.

She stopped in her tracks and momentarily stood there stock still, and so, it seemed, did her heart. Drawn as though by a force outside her jurisdiction, she found herself walking towards him.

'Hello,' she greeted him as he looked up, and for a change she didn't accompany her greeting with a smile. She felt no inclination as she normally did to be naturally pleasant or charming, and all at once it occurred to her that her defences, which she suddenly suspected were going to be the order of the day from now on when it came to any dealings she might have with this man, were right at that moment at their most vulnerable.

' 'Evening,' Quila returned briefly, rising to his feet.

He mightn't like her much, but at least he still paid her the courtesy of good manners, and this made her feel even more vulnerable. She sat down quickly on the arm of the chair in front of his. 'I thought you would have returned to Summerhaze today.'

'No.' He sat down again.

'What business can you do at the weekend?'

'None.'

Her eyes met his and even though their expression was unreadable, the depth of it made her feel as though all the air had been driven out of her body. 'Did you enjoy the show?' she asked, fighting for equanimity. She had said the first thing that had come into her head, even while knowing full well that it could well be a mistake on her part to mention her work.

That shuttered look with which she was beginning to associate with him came over his face. 'I only looked in for a minute. I had a lunch date at that hotel with a business contact,' he added with a haste that took her aback.

Then to her astonishment she detected the faintest tinge of colour darken his tan. Why, she thought, he was explaining his presence at the hotel as though he was afraid she might get the wrong idea—and obviously highly annoyed with himself for having done so. She stared at him incredulously. Could it be that he wasn't as at ease or as impervious to her as he had so cleverly led her to believe?

'And no, I did not enjoy it,' he went on as if his split second loss of composure had never occurred. 'I find the entire procedure totally repugnant. Surely any woman with half a brain in her head would find something more satisfying to do than to be a human clothes prop, to prance about half naked and be ogled at and commented on by rooms full of gormless strangers.'

Inexplicably, Romy's spirits took an upward swing and she felt suddenly that she had at least half shares in the control of the situation in which they both found themselves. She laughed outright, a frank natural laugh which as a rule she used often and easily, as she was always quick to see the humour no matter what the circumstances. 'I don't prance,' she denied, and quickly changed the subject. 'What are you reading?' She leaned forward and took his book from fingers that put up no opposition. She allowed her shoes to slip from her aching feet and drop to the floor as she studied the title. 'Jean-Paul Sartre. My goodness!' she exclaimed, looking at him in surprise. 'At this time of night?'

'Do you know Sartre?' He too sounded a little surprised.

But not as surprised as he was going to be, Romy

wagered privately. 'I studied his works extramurally while I was in New York—and I must admit, most of the study I did I did at night time, but study and reading for pleasure are two different things.' She handed him back the book.

'Why?' he asked. 'Why study Sartre?'

'Why not? I'd had my fill of Dickens and Shakespeare and the like while at school. I didn't go to university, although I would like to have, so I had to fit in what I could when I could.'

'You had a choice, I expect?'

'Between what—university or entering that puerile competition which, if I won, promised travel, glamour and excitement and a world of new experiences? Yes, I did. At eighteen the choice was scarcely a difficult one to make. I was presented with a once-in-a-lifetime opportunity, and university is hardly that. Of course I chose what I did and listened and heeded the advice of my peers which, at eighteen, one is apt to do. And I'm not at all sorry I did. As I think I implied before, I don't regret what I've done with my life, and no one has the power to make me.'

'But now it's all behind you?'

'Don't sound so cynical! I've made my decision and I intend sticking to it. I also intend not to regret that.'

'So what will you do—once the novelty of playing jam-maker and gardener at Summerhaze wears off?'

She rose an eyebrow at him. 'You should have discovered by now that I'm not easily offended.'

'I had noticed. I suppose developing a thick hide was part and parcel of your training.'

Training in which the ultimate aim, as far as he was concerned, was to be reduced to a state of inanity. Romy recognised only too well that his ambition was to rile her. 'Did you like the jam?' she asked.

'After a year of Pete's cooking, nothing would be considered an assault to the palate.'

'Well, even if I do say so myself, I'm a pretty good cook. Mum's the finest, so I had the best teacher. I enjoy cooking.'

'Are you trying to convince me that your plan now is to settle into a role of domestic bliss?'

'Oh,' Romy laughed, shaking her head and leaning towards the low table to take up the glass of ginger ale Quila had poured for her, 'believe me, I wouldn't try to convince you of anything.' There was a sparkle in her eyes as she added: 'I've made that mistake already, remember?' She took a sip of her ginger ale and over the rim of the glass she met Quila's narrowed brown eyes and although they gave nothing away, she knew intuitively that she had yet again won his interest, however reluctant, and because her intuition was so seldom wrong, she felt a sense of triumph surge within her. 'I may go to university at some stage.'

'Who or what to study this time?'

'I have no idea.'

'Do you believe in Sartre's theory?'

'Existentialism?' She shook her head. 'No. Do you?'

'Did you?' he asked, ignoring her question.

Romy shrugged lightly. 'I did consider it. But I've considered many doctrines and theories and philosophies. I was at an analytical and inquisitive age. You must have been at one time as well.'

'I still am. Aren't you?'

'Not to the same extent. Not when it comes to these subjects. I read them all up—all the isms—feverishly—Darwinism, humanism, pantheism. Even reincarnation, T.M. and the great conspiracy.' She paused on a sigh.

'So, who's arrived?' he drawled.

'I have. After revolving full circle, I've arrived back at where I began—Sunday School and a triune God.'

His eyebrows lifted at this and she could tell that she had surprised him. 'From Summerhaze to New York and from New York back to Summerhaze—you've certainly been completing some very large circles, haven't you? But why Sunday School?' He leaned back in his chair as if preparing himself for almost anything.

'It's all quite simple really,' said Romy. 'All these other doctrines have an identical aim—to wipe it out of the picture.' She cut the air with a single movement of her hand and then leaned forward, her attitude and bearing becoming tense with the seriousness of what she was saying and feeling. 'Man has always wanted to create the story, the explanation, create the creation, to take the credit, bask in the honour and glory, to be all-powerful and rich, to enslave the masses, banish freedom and individuality and finally gain total control. Who do these men think is going to save them when they really do foul things up beyond rescue?' Silence greeted her question. She blinked once or twice, aware all of a sudden of how ineffably weary she was. She straightened slowly.

'There wasn't any brandy in that glass, was there?' asked Quila.

Romy managed a half smile. 'Did I sound drunk? I must admit I'm beginning to feel a bit lightheaded.'

He smiled at her then, as though he couldn't help himself.

And even while she registered this fact, she was assailed by a peculiar breathlessness as it came to her almost simultaneously that this was the first smile he had given her. And how it altered him . . . She pulled herself together and checked her thoughts and frowned. 'Are you laughing at me?' she demanded to know.

'No. Just smiling. If you weren't swaying rather precariously on the arm of that chair, I think we could have quite a discussion, you and I.'

'I am exhausted,' Romy admitted, rather sorrowfully. Then she brightened. 'There's always tomorrow —or are you returning to Summerhaze tomorrow?'

'It's not imperative that I should.'

'Good.' She stood up and he followed suit. 'Then let's continue the argument tomorrow.'

'I didn't think we were arguing,' he said.

'No—but no doubt we will.' And lightly she touched his arm. It was an unconscious gesture. 'Goodnight.' She turned and walked away.

'Oh—Romy.'

The sound of her name on his lips debilitated her condition still further. She stopped, turned, her eyebrows raised. They lowered again when she saw her shoes being held out to her. She went back and took her shoes, having neither the power nor the courage to look up into his face. 'Silly of me,' she murmured, and with the shoes dangling from one hand, went from the room as quickly and gracefully as she could on legs that felt as though their consistency had been reduced to wax.

The weekend began and continued for Romy as though she was caught up in a dream of which she was the author, and as such she alone had the ability to make it beautiful or shatter it irreparably. Yet with each minute that came and went, she was as ignorant of the story as was Quila himself, unable to say what was to come next, knowing only that somehow the outcome was her responsibility and to make it a memorable time and keep each second as precious as the last was somehow a necessity. However, she wasn't unduly worried. The burden wasn't too great, for in fact she revelled in the challenge, the handling of something infinitely fragile and of great worth. This was the first man she had met whom she wasn't wholly sure and in total command of, and yet, conversely, the only man she wanted to bewitch as she felt sure he was, unwittingly, bewitching her. The only man with whom she lived every second of every minute and wished the minutes could be made longer.

He was as unlike the men she had become accustomed to meeting and dating as a millpond was unlike a lake that was as large, as deep and as moody as an inland sea, whose experience of women hadn't been so extensive as to make him blasé, with the attitude that all the mysteries of her sex had been uncovered and experienced so often that all that was left was a state of boredom begat by the self-indulgent philosophy by which so many lived, leaving them to wonder what all the fuss had been about.

She studied him covertly at various intervals over dinner followed by drinks on Saturday evening, and enumerated to herself the qualities she found so refreshing and so worthy of her admiration that she could forgive and even forget his bigoted attitude towards her and hope that throughout that day she had given him a more balanced glimpse into her character and caused him to revise his opinions. It was true she would like to know that she had the power to bewitch him, but she wanted even more for him to like her. He was a man of pride, self-control and depth, and with too much integrity to be governed by the fleeting, specious pleasures of the world, and yet tomorrow evening she would have to forget all these discoveries, empty her mind of every detail of this adventure and surrender him without a murmur to Julie, who had a just and prior claim.

But no—she shook back her hair, feeling it whisper over her bare shoulders. No, she wouldn't think about Julie. Julie had had an entire year, seeing him, dating him, dining with him. All she had, and was going to have, was this one day. Or maybe two . . . She brought a halt to her thoughts and sighed. She was lying, and wilfully, she knew. For if she succeeded in bewitching Quila, where would Julie figure then?

She glanced up from the lemon slice she was dunking into her Daiquiri and her eyes collided with Quila's in the narrow elongated lengths of mirrored glass which lined the wall above each of the shelves behind the house bar. Neither looked away, both still faintly circumspect. The guard was still up, Romy realised. Even though they had spent an easy day together, conversing and debating, he still hadn't fully reversed his thoughts about her. He still didn't trust her or credit her with many of the qualities he seemed to think were important in a woman. Why? 'I've enjoyed today,' she told him frankly.

'So did I,' he owned after a short pause.

'I was thinking, if we stayed another day it might give me time to earn a reprieve—even a full exoneration.'

'From what?' There was caution in his tone.

'My crime—the one I've committed in your eyes. You must admit I'm not quite the ninny you first took me for.'

'No.' A reluctant smile tugged at his attractively shaped lips. 'Not quite,' he added.

Romy pursed her lips and gave him what she hoped was a portentous look. 'I can ride a horse, lamb a ewe, make jam, bottle fruit and converse rather intelligently

on the nihilistic and pessimistic cult of Sartre; I must
have earned a place somewhere in this world,' she
pleaded, faking meekness.

Quila looked away from her and lit up a cigarette,
his third that evening.

'I didn't realise you smoked,' she commented.

'I don't, only . . .'

'Only?'

'Only on social occasions.'

Romy grinned to herself. He wasn't telling the truth;
she was sure of it. Could she be equally sure that he
was labouring under a great strain that evening in
keeping up this demeanour of perfect composure while
in her company? He wasn't at ease. She had suspected
it on several occasions earlier that evening, now she
was ready to swear by it, but there was no denying he
put up a good fight and an excellent act.

Deliberately, though applying discretion, she turned
her attention to her appearance as reflected in the mir-
rors behind the bar. From the outset she had intended
to present him with a most alluring dining companion,
while at the same time executing extreme care that she
overdid neither her make-up nor her general appearance. Never could she remember having gone to so
much trouble before for any man. The black dress with
a single narrow shoulder strap studded with minute
diamantés was simply cut and fitted her perfectly, and
although at the time she questioned the sense in purchasing it, her only acquisition from the collection she
had modelled, she was now glad she had succumbed to
temptation. Her make-up had been effectively applied,
and in the subdued lighting she met her own gaze and
wondered if her eyes appeared as deep and mysterious
to Quila as they did to her. Now that she was back
home again, it was once more becoming increasingly

difficult to manage her hair. The sun had lightened it, made it drier, and this fact, along with the softer water, caused it to spring into wild confusion. Tonight she had drawn it back off her lightly tanned face as smoothly as she could, securing it with two combs and allowing the mass of it to have its own way.

In the past the effect, if any, she might have possibly been having on the man she happened to be with had never interested her. It hadn't been important. If, tonight, Quila's equanimity was upset by her appearance and by her faintly perfumed nearness, then she was glad and for the first time felt as though she could sincerely give thanks for whatever it was about her that gave her such power.

'When do you go back to the States?' he asked suddenly.

'I don't. I've told you, I've finished.'

'It's early days yet.'

Instinct told Romy that the magical nameless quality that had preserved the day and the fragility of their new-found, perfectly in-tune footing was about to expire. She slid off the stool, an action which brought the front of her body almost against the side of his.

His head jerked around, his eyes narrowed and brilliant. For a second he looked as though he was about to say something, but his mouth, the mouth she had seen so attractively relaxed and smiling that day, remained closed, set again in the straight line she knew so well. Her heart sank.

'It's been a long day,' she said in an explanatory way.

Quila said nothing, just continued to look at her in that cold implacable manner of his. She couldn't ask him if he was staying on now, she thought in despair. He would surely say no. What *had* she done this time?

Or what had someone done a long time ago? The thought flashed like lightning through her brain, an intruder but one that brought much, if fleeting, light. Someone like her perhaps, or someone who looked like her. 'Goodnight, Quila.' She collected her silver Oroton bag, and as she started to walk away, he moved and swivelled around.

'I'll take you to your room.'

But Romy stayed him with a hand on his arm. She shook her head. 'I'll see you at breakfast.' And with her heart as heavy as stone, she walked swiftly away.

How was she going to sleep with this uncertainty hovering over her? she wondered, and while she went listlessly through the motions of preparing for bed, she began the period of speculation which she knew could well last for hours. Would he or wouldn't he stay over and spend one more day with her? She wanted him to so much, but could she bear it if she found herself continually having to ward off his barbed verbal attacks to avert unpleasantness?

CHAPTER SEVEN

AT breakfast the following morning, Quila appeared to
be in a subdued mood, and although Romy herself had
awoken refreshed and in a more optimistic frame of
mind, she felt her way cautiously, thinking that perhaps he was the type of person who didn't take kindly
to displays of heartiness first thing in the morning. He
looked and smelled fresh and shiny clean and, as
always, the sheen of his matt tanned skin drew her
attention and she found the sight of his dark curly hair,
still wet from his shower, and the smooth brown
column of his throat exposed by the open-neck style of
his blue shirt, equally attractive.

For her breakfast, Romy ordered bacon and eggs,
for she never enjoyed the dish more than when
someone else cooked it, and toast and orange juice.
'What shall we do today?' she asked casually, reaching
for a slice of the hot toast that had been set down before
her. 'Or have you decided to return to Summerhaze
this morning?'

Quila looked across at her and as usual she couldn't
even hazard a guess at what might be going through
his mind. When other men looked at her she found,
with monotonous regularity, appreciation in their
eyes and the patently obvious intention to flirt. Never
had she been met with such enigmatical directness as
Quila subjected her to. Suddenly every part of her
being was infused with the desire for him to lean over
and place that firm attractive mouth against her own.
Her longing was so intense that she felt her lips part,

as if in anticipation, even invitation.

She caught herself and looked away hurriedly, focusing her undivided attention on the triangle of toast which she began to butter.

'It's a fine day, I thought we could go for a walk this morning along the waterfront.'

An exquisite arrow of delight speared through her, but she kept her eyes lowered. 'Lovely! And perhaps this afternoon we could take in the Botanic Gardens. I haven't been up there since they installed the new cable car. It should be fun.'

His eyes flickered over the light nature of her V-necked T-shirt, horizontally striped in colours of khaki, cream and lemon to team up with the khaki colour of her fashion slacks. 'It may be fine, but there's sure to be a cool breeze blowing in off the harbour.'

'Don't worry,' Romy assured him happily. 'I have a sweater.'

The walk along the city's scenic waterfront was undertaken with only snatches of conversation being exhanged between the two of them. It very soon became apparent that Quila's disinclination to talk was to carry on from breakfast. Not that Romy minded, for she felt it was an easy silence and she could relax more fully when they weren't speaking and enjoy uninhibitedly the beauty of the morning, the sparkling blue harbour protectively encircled by mountainous green and blue hills etched against a paler blue sky. The world seemed to be painted either blue or green and lit by a bright pale gold sun, the heat of which was muted considerably by the ever-present wind Quila had mentioned whipping up off the surface of the water. She tied her sweater about her shoulders and lifted her face to the buffeting breeze, looking forward to the next time she would bump into Quila or he would brush against her.

After a light lunch of filled rolls and fruit consumed on the slopes of the Botanic Gardens which overlooked the city and harbour below, Quila lay back on the sweating, sweet-smelling grass, and instead of dozing off as Romy half expected him to do, his urge to converse seemed to have been resuscitated. 'Are you missing the States?' he asked.

Still in a sitting position, with her arms linked loosely about her knees, Romy looked over her shoulder at him. Contrary to her expectations, his eyes weren't closed but were directed straight at her. She shrugged. 'A little. I miss my friends, of course. Do you?'

'I guess my answer is the same as yours.'

'Do you intend returning?'

'No.' The answer was prompt and positive.

'Leon told me you managed the farm neighbouring his father's in Iowa for a number of years.'

'So I did.'

'Had you farmed at all before then?'

'I grew up on a farm.'

'When did you go to the States?' she continued to question, though finding it a wearying business. To exact information from him about himself was like pulling teeth!

'When I was young, like you. And like you I've returned. But unlike you, the life I want is here. I have no intention of going back.'

Romy held his gaze, her own becoming as unyielding and as steady as his own. 'I realise you don't give me much credit for anything, least of all any ability for knowing my own mind, but I don't want an argument. It's too lovely a day, so let's change the subject.'

Quila folded his hands beneath his head. 'How about sport—an innocuous enough topic. Did you ever go skiing at Aspen?'

She grimaced and relaxed, reclining back on the grass, supporting herself on one arm. 'No, not at Aspen. My one and only experience of skiing was at Lake Placid, and it's an experience I wouldn't care to repeat. Skiing is definitely not for me.'

'Why?' asked Quila, grinning all over his face as though he had already conjured up a picture of the event and a highly coloured one at that. 'What happened?'

'Wipe that grin off your face or I won't tell you.'

He assumed an expression of serious interest. 'How's that!'

'Mmm, passable,' she conceded in a tone that conveyed she was being extremely forbearing. 'Well, skiing proved to be quite a revelation to me in more ways than one. I discovered for the first time that I was frightened to death of heights, and I was the only one in my party who was frightened to death of heights and yet still expected to go up the mountain as all the others did, on a T-bar. I feel faint now even thinking about it. I simply couldn't do it, so I was left to go up on the chairlift—alone. I think those mountains must still be ringing with my screams. I'll never forget those huge gaping chasms or the eerie silence—when I wasn't screaming, that is, to reassure myself that I hadn't died of fright. When I'd recovered sufficiently so that my legs didn't continue to give out on me, I began my first skiing lesson. It began and ended in disaster. I'm sure everyone there was quietly relieved when I gave up.'

'I thought you'd have had greater perseverance than

that,' he commented. 'Imagine giving in after only one lesson!'

'If what happened to me could happen to you, you'd have given up too.'

He began grinning again. 'What did happen?'

Romy pulled up a handful of grass and threw it in his face and grinned ruefully. 'Well, aside from skiing straight through someone's picnic area, one of my skis, the left one, got stopped by a mogul, I think they called it, while my right ski carried right on going, and I sat down so heavily on my bindings I was left feeling as though I'd ridden a horse bareback clean across the continent.'

Quila had begun to roar with laughter almost before she had ended her account, and in a display of mocked pique that he should find the thought of her past misfortune so hilarious, Romy pulled up more handsful of grass and leaned across and rubbed them into his face.

'You should consider yourself fortunate,' he told her, sobering and ridding his face and mouth and shirt of the remnants of grass. 'At least you didn't ski off the mountain.'

'Ski *off* the mountain? How can anyone possibly ski off a mountain?'

'Well, I certainly managed it,' he told her.

'You? Skiied off a mountain?' She eyed him sceptically. 'When? Where?'

'Years ago. Off Mount Ruaphehu during a white-out.'

'Well, what on earth were you doing, skiing during a white-out? Even *I* wouldn't have been that stupid!'

'I wasn't skiing during a white-out,' he explained with exaggerated patience. 'When I began skiing the weather wasn't excellent, but my view wasn't hindered in any way. One second it was clear, the next I couldn't

see a damn thing. I remembered thinking how soft the
snow felt all of a sudden, and after falling a good
twenty-five feet, I discovered why.'

'How terrifying!' Romy didn't know whether to gasp
or giggle. 'But you were all right?'

'I was dashed against some rocks and knocked out to
it for a while. When I came to and realised that my
yells for help must have been as puny as a squeak from
a mouse in the basement of a New York skyscraper
hoping to be heard by a mate in the penthouse, I had
to accept that the only person who could help me was
me.'

'So what did you do?'

'Walked. After three hours I came to a trampers'
hut and found a log book which helpfully informed me
that I had at least another two and a half hour hike
still ahead of me before I came out on to the road.'

Romy groaned with heartfelt sympathy. 'Then
what?'

'After heating up a can of soup and scraping the
edges off some mouldy cheese which someone had
kindly left behind, I pressed bravely on.'

'And all this walking was done in your ski boots?'

'What else? I could scarcely dart home and change,
could I?'

'And you made it to the road?'

'And lived to tell the tale.'

'How long did you have to wait until someone came
along and picked you up?'

'Not long, actually. And by a carload of smart-alecs,
as it happened, who took one sweeping look at me in
my ski gear, carrying my poles and skis, with the
mountain miles away in the distance, totally concealed
by cloud, and enquired: "Have you lost something,
mate?" '

At this, Romy's sympathy turned out to be very shortlived indeed. Her imagination proved to be just as fertile as his and his misadventure unfurled before her mind's eye in both cinemascope and Technicolor. The initial tentative giggles soon evolved into gales of laughter and she fell back on the grass, soon having to seek relief by holding her protesting stomach muscles.

When finally she sobered, she turned her head to gaze at him through the stems of dandelions, daisies and blades of grass. He was grinning at her, offended in no way by her mirth at his expense.

He propped himself up on one elbow and as he did so, Romy was visited by the same all-consuming longing as she had been at breakfast. She wanted him to kiss her, yearned to feel the touch of his mouth as she had never yearned for the touch of any man's lips. And she felt her face begin to reflect her desire. Her mouth and cheeks grew warm and her eyes darkened and became heavy. She sat up abruptly so that her back was to him and began fiddling with her hair, releasing it from the clip into which it had been gathered only to secure it more severely than it had been before. Silence fell between them, and Romy was glad of it.

It was Quila who eventually broke it. 'What made you want to arrange a party for those children—I.H.C. children, I think Leon said?'

Romy looked over her shoulder at him, hoping that she appeared more composed than she felt. Not that it mattered, for this time his eyes were closed. She shrugged slightly. 'Yes, they were intellectually handicapped. And it wasn't a party, it was a picnic, and neither was it something new. Before I went overseas we use to arrange similar occasions every year, Kit and Sean, my cousins, and my mother.' She reclined back once more and balanced herself on one arm and picked the nearby daisies as she spoke. 'It was fun. But things at Summerhaze have changed so much compared to the way they were before I left, but I thought that with Leon's assistance I could at least try to revive one of the traditions that have been let go and restore some of the old life and gaiety we used to have. And it worked. I know Mum and Pop enjoyed feeding the multitudes and seeing the place being used to make the children happy.'

Quila had opened his eyes as she was talking and he looked at her now. 'And did you?'

'Of course. If Summerhaze belonged to me, I'd fill all its rooms with children.'

'With intellectually handicapped children?'

'No, with my own.'

She had the pleasure of seeing him nonplussed. But it was only a fleeting victory for her, for his surprise very quickly turned into derision. 'You really should try your hand at writing stories. You'd come up with some very original yarns, I'm sure.'

'Oh, come on, Quila,' she protested, 'be fair! Do I ever scoff at you for what you say? Whatever else you may think of me, I'm not a liar.'

'No, well, I suppose you're pretty safe nurturing that ambition, since it's never likely to eventuate.'

'No, about that you're probably right!' she snapped at him. She'd never let him know how much he had pained her. 'But tell me, what do you think of the idea?'

'What idea? Of you filling the rooms of Summerhaze with your chidren?'

'No, I mean the idea of the rooms of Summerhaze being filled with children.'

He was silent for a moment. 'I couldn't wish the old homestead a better fate,' he said quietly, and Romy recognised it to be a sincere reply.

'A better fate than to fall under an axe?'

Quila sat up abruptly, the look he swung at her sharp and alert. 'What do you mean?'

She hesitated, but only for a split second, then blurted: 'Just that if you're entertaining any ideas of marrying Julie and filling Summerhaze with *your* children, then you'd better think again. Julie hates Summerhaze and hates country life, but while she might be quite prepared to tolerate country life if she were to marry you, Summerhaze itself she'd never suffer. Think on that!'

His eyes had narrowed and had become even narrower as she spoke. When she had come to the end of her little diatribe, he lay back on the grass once more, an enigmatic quirk tugging at the corners of his mouth.

Romy shivered suddenly. What was he thinking? What a shockingly disloyal, vindictive sister Julie had been blessed with? She grappled frantically through her mind. God, what had she said?

'But you would be prepared to "suffer" the old homestead?'

Romy tossed her head and declined to answer, furiously angry and disgusted with herself for having let her tongue run away with her like that. What a grossly idiotic thing to do!

'Wouldn't you like to see Summerhaze pulled down and a lovely modern mansion erected in its place?' he persisted.

Her eyes blazed at him. 'No! I love Summerhaze— just as it is.'

'But not so Julie?'

Romy lowered her eyes to the daisies in her hand and compressed her lips.

'Don't worry,' Quila drawled lazily. 'You haven't revealed any secrets that weren't already quite obvious to me. I realised immediately that you and Julie were as different as night and day. And I also know that Julie can't stand a bar of the place. What puzzles me is why you should profess to love it.'

'I don't *profess* to love it. I do love it. And why shouldn't I? It's my home. And I love old things.'

'And young things, too—like children?'

'Yes. What's so odd about that?'

'Nothing. I just wonder what you would do once the novelty of the quiet life and motherhood at Summerhaze wore thin.'

'It wouldn't wear thin. It's what I've always wanted and dreamed about.'

'When?'

'When what?'

'When did you dream about it? When you were living it up in London or Rome? Or was it when you were swinging your shapely hips and flashing your long legs along some catwalk in Paris, or pouting sexily for some photographer in New York . . .?'

'Stop it!' she all but shouted at him. 'Stop deriding and ridiculing me every chance you get. I'm sick and tired of it! Do you hear me?'

'I hear you,' he returned dryly. 'As did everyone in the Botanic Gardens, I imagine.'

'You think *I'm* despicable!' she hissed. '*You're* the one who's despicable!'

'If you thought about it you'd see I was doing you a favour,' he pointed out.

'Oh, really? And how do you make that out? Or perhaps I'd be better off if I didn't ask,' she muttered belatedly.

'Some women are born for the home life, caring for

a husband and family. Others, like yourself, are better suited to decorative purposes, adorning the covers of magazines and . . .'

'And walls of shearers' quarters,' Romy finished for him, glaring at him. Their gazes clashed and held, like those of two combatants, one watching the other, both waiting for the other's next move. It was Quila who spoke and moved first.

'You can't honestly expect me to believe that you've even considered spoiling one line or one curve of that beautiful body of yours through the distorting process of childbearing.'

While Romy had long since reached the conclusion that nothing he said could possibly shock her now, she never for a moment dreamed that he would touch her. But she actually saw his hand reach out and certainly didn't imagine the feather-like caress of his fingers over the peaked tip of one breast. She gasped, reacting instinctively by pulling back and sitting up. 'Don't—do that!'

'Then wear a bra. You're inviting to be touched.' He had lain back on the grass with his hands folded beneath his head once more. His eyes surveyed her lazily and she knew she was colouring in spite of herself.

'You're obsessed with bras!' she snapped.

'Not with bras but probably, like most men, I have to claim to having a healthy interest in that part of the woman's anatomy that should be wearing one.'

'I *am* wearing one!' So exclaiming, she reached for her sweater and pulled it on. 'You're churlish, crude—and a boor!' she enunciated, trying vainly to still the trembling of her lips. 'I'm going for a walk, and if I'm not back by the time you want to leave—go without me!' And scrambling to her feet, she stalked off.

She got as far as the children's playground and sat down rather unsteadily on one of the swings. She was close to tears and totally oblivious to the commotion being made by the few children who still remained at this, the end of the sunny afternoon. Why did Quila have to spoil everything? she wondered bleakly. He *always* spoiled everything. She moved restlessly, rose from the swing and moved from one item of children's equipment to another, running her hand unconsciously over their smooth, now cold surfaces. At first she had longed for him to kiss her, but that longing had expanded as the intimate caress of his fingers had revealed. How could she possibly feel like this about such a man? And why? What was it about him that made her long to be crushed against him, for his weight to bear down on her and still the restlessness of her limbs and assuage this new dull ache within her body?

'Romy?'

She started, almost out of her skin. Spinning around, she stood facing Quila, her fists bunched and her body taut and poised as though for flight. Eyes that shimmered warily held his.

'I'd like to apologise,' he said quietly. 'I went too far.'

'Way too far,' she agreed stiltedly, still unable to relax. 'You always do.'

'I know. And I'm sorry.' He paused. 'May I take you to dinner to help atone?' he asked, a little diffidently.

'Dinner? But don't you have to get back to Summerhaze?'

'I'm an early riser.' He extended a hand to her. 'Truce?'

Her hesitation was but a token display of resistance. Romy nodded, knowing that deep down she was overjoyed to hear him utter that word, but that it would take an hour or so for it to rise to the surface. With a solemn little smile she slipped her cool slim hand into his larger, work-roughened one and at once wanted more—to slip into his embrace, to know what it was like to feel that calloused hand against her softer, more sensitive skin, and she knew that in future everything that he did in relation to her was going to evoke within her such thoughts and feelings as she was now experiencing.

That evening slipped smoothly and quietly by with neither of them seeming to feel the need to talk. They ate out at a recommended restaurant and strolled back to the hotel side by side along the wharf front, listening to the throb of the ships' engines, the lap of water against their hulls and the occasional raucous laughter and snatches of conversation in Russian, Japanese and German floating from the ships' crews.

Not once did Quila make any attempt to touch her, but Romy was not dismayed. She knew that he would, simply by the way he would look at her and their eyes would meet. Nothing had been said, but she knew that she would learn what it was like to be in his arms before the evening ended. And so did he. Meanwhile, there was no hurry.

Somewhere in the narrow, dimly lit corridor between the lift and her room, she felt his first touch on her bare skin and she responded without thought. The coming together of their bodies was like two sighs breathed in unison, their lips met without preliminary and his kiss was all that she had suspected it would be and more. A soft moan, almost of pain, escaped him as he wrapped his arms more fully about her, bringing her closer, holding her more tightly. His kisses owned a desperate, almost pleading quality that confused as

well as excited her. It seemed as though he needed,
was begging something of her which she didn't understand and could only offer a total response and make
him aware that her hunger and need matched his own.

Eventually he lifted his head and Romy followed the
withdrawal of his mouth from hers until she was raised
up on her toes. Then reluctantly she left the haven of
his arms, aware only of the heat beating in her face
and the jerky, unco-ordinated movements of her limbs
as she moved across to the door to her room and
fumbled for her key. Her actions halted abruptly when
she looked up to see Quila, his breathing still heavy,
lean back against the wall beside her door and a sheen
of perspiration having gathered over his forehead and
across the top of his upper lip. Wonderingly, she
reached out and ran her fingers over the more abrasive
skin, delighting in the excuse for such intimate contact.
Her caress was cut short as his hand came up to clamp
around her wrist. He glanced at her briefly, deeply,
before pressing his lips for a long moment into the
palm of her hand.

'Where's your key?' he asked harshly, abruptly pulling her hand down from his lips.

Silently she found it and handed it to him, and he
swiftly unlocked the door and drew her into the room
as though he had actually done so every night of their
sojourn at the hotel.

Time to switch on the wall lamps was allowed her,
but she had to let her clutch purse slip to the floor as
Quila brought her into his arms in a way she couldn't
have resisted even if she had wanted to. Held close
against him, she felt a trembling originating from deep
within him, and marvelled. Other men had trembled
in her arms, but they had not been of Quila's calibre,
and possibly that was why she had no difficulty in

recognising their excitement to be of an ephemeral and superficial nature emanating not from the hitherto sleeping untouched core of their beings.

In the past, on realising this, she had felt a withdrawal within herself and a desire to bring to an end all physical contact, but this was a difference she had never experienced, and when she became aware of being lowered to her bed, she made no demur but caught her breath as his body, its muscles taut and movements restrained, came to rest gently on hers.

She gloried in the feel of him, heavy and warm and vital, fitting to the contours of her body as though he had been created specifically for her. Snaking her arms up around his neck and the width of his hard muscled back, she brought his head down to hers, longing once more for the touch of his mouth upon her own. For some moments he seemed strangely intent on denying her, disciplining his lips to stillness on hers until the seduction of hers and the final quicksilver touch of her tongue unleashed a response that she wasn't sure she had the fortitude to equal.

Eventually the assault on her mouth become less tumultuous and more exhortive, seeking and drawing a response of which she hadn't known she was capable, and it seemed as though she had waited a lifetime to feel this way, as though even a full and total response wasn't enough to give this man. Rendered faint and short of breath by her heightened senses, she was at last forced to free her mouth. Turning aside her hot, flushed face, she curled her fingers until they were clutching at his shirt. She felt his lips lower to linger against the side of her neck and press along her throat and his hands besought and caressed her until of its own accord her body rose against his for even closer contact.

'Quila!' At the touch of his hand on the soft skin beneath her strappy, deep rose pink T-shirt, the name was ejected on a gasp and smothered by his mouth once more claiming her own with a passion that echoed within her and threatened to overwhelm them both.

It was very gradual, the growing awareness that she was somehow caught, hampered, the movement of her head impeded, restricting her responses. Frustrated, she moaned and pushed at Quila until, reluctantly it seemed, he became conscious of her need to be free of his weight. When at last his body had lifted, she lay quite still thinking that at any minute her body, which suddenly felt so cool and weightless, would float away. Eventually, with hands that were none too steady, she struggled to disentangle the hairclip which had become enmeshed and had her firmly linked with the cotton lace counterpane.

Sitting up, she drew one leg up under her and raised her arms to proceed to pull the clips from her hair and allow it to tumble freely over her shoulders, shaking it back from her face. She reached across and dropped the pins on the bedside table, then looked at Quila, who lay back on the bed with his head pillowed on one arm, and all the apprehension she had begun to feel about what the result might be of the interruption she had been responsible for immediately slipped away as she sighted his face, its heightened colour and his eyes on her, slumbrous and uncommonly bright.

'You're beautiful,' he said in a voice husky and so unlike his own. His hand lifted to touch her hair, then proceeded to glide upward to cradle the side of her face.

Although at no time had she seen registered on his face the total depth of the emotion she had felt seething within him, she now sensed an intensity she had never encountered in any man. Incapable of a reply, she answered by the only means she considered would be appropriate. Turning her face, she pressed a kiss into his palm, then another along the inside of his wrist.

With eyes heavy and languorous, she looked down into his, the depths of which were darker and somehow even more fathomless, and her prior uncertainty of him extended to incorporate herself. Never had she dreamed she could feel this way, for the emotion Quila had awakened within her had, up until then, lain dormant—but was it enough?

She guessed instinctively that he was less experienced than many of the men she had been used to associating with, but unlike them he would, in love, be capable of giving all of himself. He would never do anything by halves. This was the kind of man she wanted, the kind of man she had been unconsciously waiting for. But now that she had found him, she was afraid. Just how great was her capacity? Quila would love grandly, wonderfully, wholly and totally. But could she? And not disappoint him? Or would she prove as inadequate as he had caused her to begin to believe that late afternoon by the river's edge?

'Romy,' Quila murmured, not without a hint of scorn. 'How did you ever come by such a name?'

Romy sank down beside him and, desiring more contact with him than simply the touch of his fingers caressing the nape of her neck, she ensured that her front came to rest lightly against his side. The mere anticipation of the closer, crushing contact for which she had yearned and which would later be restored was pleasurable in itself. Leaning on one elbow, she looked down at him, mildly rebuking. 'Well, yours isn't exactly of the John, David or Stephen variety!'

'That's where you're wrong.'

Romy raised her eyebrows at him. 'Quila?'

'Aquila, actually, arising from the very same source as John, David and Stephen.'

She pondered for a few moments and then offered tentatively: 'The Bible?'

'Aquila Daniel,' he supplied dryly. 'Two good solid Old Testament names decided upon by my eminent mother—though how or when she ever came to experience the urge to open up a Bible, I'll never know.'

The wealth of bitterness with which he uttered the words stunned Romy. Her gaze on his face became transfixed. She wanted to ask him what he meant by such a remark, but although in her mind she knew all the right words, she couldn't summon the appropriate formats for the questions she desired to ask. Hesitantly, she lifted a hand to run her fingers gently over the once more tautened line of the mouth which earlier she had been solely responsible for softening.

Swiftly he caught her hand in a tight grip, pressed a hard brief kiss on the tips of her fingers and pulled her hand down to rest on his chest. 'Well,' he said, quirking an eyebrow at her. 'Your turn.'

'I think my mother was quite enamoured of a German film star who featured in some movie she saw at the time I was born, so I was named after her.'

Quila's eyes bored into hers for several long moments, then he said quietly: 'There's no getting away from it, is there? Named after a film star, for God's sake! You were doomed right from the start.'

'Don't be absurd,' she retorted mildly. 'You're named after Daniel. Does that make you a prophet?'

'Perhaps—when it comes to picturing what's ahead for you.'

'Oh?' she smiled teasingly. 'Then, pray, tell me my future.'

'Prophet or no prophet, that wouldn't be difficult to forecast. Imminent boredom, a consequent return to a way of life which exerts a hold over women similar to the hold heroin has over a drug addict and which, like all such addictions, brings initial euphoria followed by a steady decline and ultimate destruction.'

'My goodness!' Romy exclaimed with contrived horror. 'Such impending doom! You should have been named after Jeremiah.'

An expression bordering on a scowl came over Quila's features and an imp of mischief in Romy compelled her to tease him still further. 'Star quality!' she declared solemnly, looking away and waving her hand as though across an imaginary display of lights which spelt out her name. ' "Romy Palliser! She has it all!" That's what they said,' she told him, turning to look at Quila once more. 'I had "star quality". As a model I could be so many different things—gay, piquant, haunting, winsome, alluring, seductive, innocent.' And with each adjective, she struck an exaggerated pose and simulated each portrayal. She laughed finally and relaxed beside him once more. 'Now I'll let you in on a secret. For all that "star quality", once out of the studio, "blank" is me, the real me. I'd catch a glimpse of myself in the mirror sometimes and think: "You're a fraud, Romy Palliser. Your face is as dead as a pan." '

'Believe me, your face is never blank or dead when you're talking,' Quila responded sourly, 'which is most of the time.'

Romy made a move with her mouth. 'If you don't want me to retaliate in self-defence then you shouldn't provoke me,' she muttered and, almost without thinking, moved up over the side of him until she was able to take delight in touching his brooding eyes with her lips, then the side of his face, his ear and the smooth brown column of his neck which she found so attractive, tasting the roughened salty texture of his skin with her tongue. A long shudder swept through him, reverberating against her, and his hands came to grip her back with a sense of urgency.

'Romy. Romy!' She hadn't needed his second bidding to bring her mouth to his, and yet still he had seemed compelled to repeat her name against her lips.

Sliding her fingers up into his hair, she removed her mouth from his and, with his head in her hands, caressed his face with her lips until, with a stifled groan, he executed a swift manoeuvre which transposed their positions. For the only time in her life, Romy gave of herself without thought or compunction and allowed herself to be swept away in a man's embrace. It came to her gradually, the realisation that Quila was the one taking responsibility for what would usually have been her duty, and in her place, exerted control. His kisses became more and more restrained and the intimate searching of his hands didn't even resume.

With expanding amazement, she opened her eyes and studied the somewhat strained countenance above hers. Had she relaxed and surrendered herself so completely because some intuition had already whispered to her that Quila would not try to make love to her unless she indicated quite specifically that that was her wish? Or did he consider she behaved in such a manner as this with all the men she dated? Her mind recoiled from the contemplation of this possibility. The opportunity, the luxury, and only with Quila could it be described as such, had never before been hers, whereby she had experienced such powerful emotions and was afforded the chance to express them. Surely it indicated emotional, not only physical involvement on Quila's part? It had been wonderful, and she wanted to give herself totally to this man and only to him, but she needed no one to advise her that it would be wrong and would undoubtedly spoil something new and precious that had sprung up between them. She didn't want to spoil anything. 'You're not going to attempt to make love to me, are you?' she asked quietly.

'Is that what you want?' The throbbing quality of his speech made her senses leap.

'And you don't?'

'That's a silly bloody question.' He drew away from her and fell back on the bed.

Raising herself up on one elbow, she looked down at him and smiled, and an onrush of tender emotion made her rash and in an unthinking effort to relieve the tension between them, she said flippantly: 'And to think you were a man who claimed that he didn't go for females with bird-size brains, outsized egos and wall-to-wall teeth!'

The silence which ensued hadn't even begun before Romy realised that she had made a colossal faux pas. Quila's eyes had grown suddenly cold and Romy couldn't suppress the shiver at this swift foreboding change that had come over him.

'So.' His voice, though still ragged from the on-slaught of previous emotions, now had a bleak edge to it. 'That's what's behind this. I'd forgotten how easily all of this sort of thing comes to the likes of you. Is your ego so fragile that you have to prove to yourself that no man is immune? Or is it the game you enjoy?'

Shocked, Romy couldn't believe what she was hearing, much less think of a coherent reply. She watched him drag himself up into a sitting position on the edge of the bed and begin to pull on his shoes.

'Quila,' she pleaded huskily, sitting up and touching the hard muscled shoulder. He flinched away immediately and her hand sprang back as though it had come into contact with fire. 'You've misconstrued what I said, misunderstood everything about me.'

'You reckon?' He was standing now, the familiar derision tainting his features, though now it was mixed with a liberal quantity of weariness. 'I've wanted to kiss you probably from the first time I saw you, but I was glad the opportunity to do so never arose, because I knew I'd be disappointed. And how right I was . . .'

'Quila!' Romy gasped, as though in pain, for he had indeed lashed out at her in the only way that had the power at that moment to hurt her. 'That's a lie!' She was up on her knees on the bed, her voice ringing out full of the conviction she felt when she recalled the film of perspiration she had touched on his face in the corridor following their initial embrace. 'You can say that now because for some strange warped reason of your own, that's what you want to believe.'

'Is it? You're just a shell, Romy, pretty, empty, superficial. How many times have you played this game? How many men have you managed to make fall under your spell and dance to your tune? You're all the same; how could I have even entertained the thought that you might be different?'

Nothing was going to alter his mind or attitude now, Romy could see that clearly, and she grew increasingly frustrated and angry, both with herself and him. 'How can any reasonably intelligent man possibly say that all women are the same?' she raged at him.

'I didn't mention women,' he said, perplexing and angering her further. And slinging his jacket over one shoulder, he left her room without another word.

Experiencing an overwhelming urge to throw something, Romy gave in to it by hurling first one of her shoes at the closed door and then the other. Her agitation, however, didn't decrease as a result of her indulging frustration. He was a coward as well as a liar! she fumed to herself. He seemed unable to admit to or take responsibility for his emotions, emotions that she alone aroused in him, someone whom, when it suited him, he could obviously and conveniently forget he despised.

It was some time later before her eyes actually saw the image of herself reflected in the long mirror above the dressing-table opposite, and the anguish she was feeling whitening her face. Quila had hurt her this time, the realisation came to her. Now she cared and could no longer shrug it off. Now she should hate him—but it was far too late for that.

Did he really consider her a butterfly who flitted from one attractive flowerbed to another? Her smile resembled a grimace. The first time she had even come close to losing her head, and she had to blow everything. How ironical! But even if she hadn't so much as opened her mouth she would have managed to blow it by just being who she was—Romy Palliser, ex-model. Why?

The question pounded unanswered around in her brain as, both physically and emotionally exhausted, she lay down on the bed. Shivering uncontrollably, she pulled the counterpane, still warm from their bodies, up over her shoulders. When, some hours later, she awoke chilled and uncomfortable, she quickly changed into her nightdress and spent the remainder of the night sleeping a troubled, fitful sleep between the sheets.

CHAPTER EIGHT

THE following morning, Romy enquired and was informed that Quila Morgan had checked out late the night before which, to Romy, could only have been taken to mean that he had considered any endeavour to fit in a restful night before the eighty-mile journey to Summerhaze a waste of time, and this conclusion mollified her to a certain extent.

Over a leisurely yet meagre breakfast, she came to a decision which injected some speed and purpose into her movements. Nellie, his aunt and a lifelong friend of her family, would surely be able to throw some light on to the subject. But the question was—would she? She was a woman who kept her own counsel and took her loyalties and responsibilities seriously, and in this case her first loyalty would lie with her own flesh and blood.

As always, the older woman was delighted to see Romy and promptly insisted that she stay for lunch, which Nellie had already decided to have out at the table on the back brick courtyard beneath the shade of the old plum tree. Romy accepted the invitation with alacrity, for she had no desire now to hurry back to Summerhaze where Quila was such a prominent feature. She put a call through to her mother to explain that she would be arriving home later that afternoon and then set about helping Nellie prepare a salad for lunch, chatting to her about the events that had taken place in Wellington the week before. And although she avoided, for the time being at least, all mention of her meetings with Quila, Nellie herself introduced the subject by asking if she had by chance bumped into him.

The question was asked innocently enough, but with Nellie one could never tell whether she had touched upon the subject which was uppermost in one's mind accidentally or at the prompting of her remarkable perspicacity.

'Yes, I did see Quila,' she replied casually. 'It just so happened he was staying at the same hotel as I'd been booked into.' As nonchalantly as she was able, Romy spread the green and white checked tablecloth over the outside table and began transferring on to it the contents of the tray she had set down on one of the chairs.

'Did you tell him why you were in Wellington?'

'Yes, I did, and he even poked his head in one afternoon to have a look, much to my surprise.' She looked up from her task and caught a glimpse of that same surprise in Nellie's expression. 'I see it's amazed you, too.'

'It has. One doesn't expect a man like Quila, with a background like his, to go to a fashion parade,' Nellie replied, and then chuckled.

'He was only there for five minutes—if that.' Romy paused, then plunged on in what she hoped was a conversational manner, pushing unnecessarily at the knife and fork which she had already correctly placed: 'What is his background, Nellie?'

'Now why should that be of interest to you? Oh, I see I've forgotten the salad dressing. What would you like, Romy? French or mayonnaise?'

Romy stifled a sigh. 'French, thanks, Nellie.'

'The reason I'm interested in Quila's background, Nellie,' Romy was obliged to reintroduce the subject once Nellie had returned with the dressing since she obviously had no intention herself of referring to it again, 'is because of his attitude towards me, not only in Wellington but at Summerhaze, from the very minute I arrived home.'

'Attitude? What kind of attitude?'

'Strange—no, to be perfectly truthful, I'd have to describe it as being downright hostile. At first I couldn't understand why, then as it continued I was able to link it to the fact that I was a model—or rather an ex-model, a status he refuses to accept.'

'Mmmm.' Nellie passed her the freshly tossed salad, comprised of lettuce, tomatoes, cucumber and spring onions. 'Are you sure you're not imagining all this?'

'No, of course I'm not imagining it. I was hoping you'd be able to throw some light on the matter, help me understand the man.' A tinge of frustration had entered Romy's voice and, hearing it for herself, she inhaled deeply and tried to restore her former air of indifference.

'Good heavens, what does it matter to you what his opinion of you is? I'm sure you're more than capable of putting him in his place.'

'So I am,' Romy replied with forced lightness, applying the tongs to lift a generous slice of ham. 'But that doesn't stop me from wanting to understand.'

Nellie shrugged. 'Perhaps there's nothing *to* understand. Perhaps he doesn't like you—as simple as that. You've no doubt been used to having men fall all over themselves to land at your feet, and it's now nettling you to find one man who won't oblige you by behaving the same way.'

'It's not that at all!' Romy denied strongly.

'Then I suggest you forget it, and if it's Quila you're worried about, and his unsociable manners, then don't. He's a surly cuss—always has been.'

Romy's eyes widened in amazement. 'You sound as though you don't like him.'

Nellie greeted this speculation with a hoot of laughter. 'He can be exceedingly infuriating, I grant you, but for all that, I love him dearly.'

Romy relaxed visibly.

'As does Julie.'

At this she stiffened, just as noticeably.

'Or at least she imagines she does,' and with that, Nellie spooned a large dollop of mustard pickle on to the side of her plate.

Romy's gaze on the indomitable face, lined with character and beauty, was unwavering. 'You—you don't think she does?'

'*I* can say that I don't think she does. But when *you* are the one imagining yourself in love, then in love you are, for as long as it lasts. It would be a pity for them both if they were to marry, though. They're not right for one another.'

Romy felt her heart, which had begun to plummet at the beginning of this interchange, drop still further. She swallowed, then managed with commendable aplomb: 'So you think they will marry? That must mean Quila is in love with Julie.'

'Quila, as far as I know, has loved only one woman—his mother, and she managed to turn that very precious love into loathing and disgust. I doubt if he knows what love is all about. He's never had any, and if he could learn to trust and respect a woman, and he does trust and respect Julie, then I'm sure for him that would be enough—more than enough. If you want to save him from committing the folly of marrying Julie, who could never love him to the extent he needs—whether he knows it or not—to be loved, then you'll have to prove to him that you are indeed an "ex-model".'

The heat was coming and going in tides over Romy's body like waves washing up and fanning out over the seashore. She was quivering all over and had to rest her knife and fork down on her plate and look away towards the garden to blink back the sudden film of moisture which had blurred her vision. As she wiped and twisted her clammy hands on the serviette spread over her lap, she felt Nellie's hand rub up and down her back. 'You were tricking me,' Romy accused tremulously, 'all along.'

'Not really,' Nellie said kindly. 'It was what I began to hope for from the moment you returned home and I recognised you standing at my gate. Besides, I'm an old woman. It wasn't difficult for me to realise why you'd come to see me.' Then after a pause: 'Do you love him, Romy? Do you really love him?'

Romy sighed, then nodded. 'I think so—though why I don't know. It would be far easier to hate him, he's so condemnatory of me, so arrogantly sure and so smug and self-righteous in all his opinions. I'd like to hit him!'

'But end up kissing him instead,' Nellie concluded dryly.

Romy felt warmth rise in her face, but managed to laugh good-humouredly and relax a little. 'All right, Nellie, I concur you've won the day, but please don't persist in embarrassing me by hammering home your advantage.' All the same, she was relieved a little, for now that all was out in the open, she could proceed to ask Nellie any questions she wanted to, and all as pointed as she cared to make them.

As she drove slowly on out to Summerhaze, she pondered on all that Nellie had told her. How cold she had gone, swamped with foreboding, when she had learned that Quila's mother had, like her, been a model before her marriage and, like her, had chased success to America. The essential difference was that Geraldine Morgan had never surrendered her love of the glamour which had been part and parcel of the occupation and had deserted her husband and child to recapture it. Nellie had supposed that at nineteen, Geraldine had been too young to be expected to exchange her up-and-coming career in modelling in Auckland for one of domesticity on a farm in Northland. But having fallen pregnant, and enamoured of her lover who had, in her eyes, been more of a challenge and more masculine than his city counterparts, she had agreed to marriage. However, she had soon tired of the isolation of being a farmer's wife and the bondage in which her dependent child placed her and had begun to hunger for the bright lights of the city and for the fickle limelight which could quickly forget her and become focused on new and just as pretty faces and figures.

Spending much of her time in the city, away from her husband and child, as she did, it wasn't long before an offer was made to her to go to Australia. Quila had been five when she left and seven when his father remarried. Geraldine had darted back and forth across the Tasman quite regularly to visit her son and each time attempts to mollify the boy after she had left had become less and less successful. Eventually she had stopped coming altogether.

Throughout the ensuing years, she wrote him the occasional letter from America, but even they too had gradually ceased, leaving him to develop an indifference to his stepmother and a growing hatred for his father who, it seemed only logical to him, must have not wanted his mother at all, for he had married again without having made any attempt to fetch her back. Quila had grown up beside his one half-brother and sister, determined to learn all he could and leave as soon as he could to find and join his mother.

At barely eighteen, he left New Zealand and by the time he was nineteen he had found her, but soon after his discovery came another. Geraldine Morgan was not at all the wronged woman he had conjured her up to be in his mind. She wasn't even as beautiful as he remembered her or as depicted in the earlier photos which he had rescued and coveted from the garden incinerator where his father had tossed them. Although she had taken him in and seemed, initially at least, proud to find herself in possession of such a fine-looking son, the facts he had subsequently learned about her had not been pleasant ones. Nonetheless, he had stuck by her, for he had been at a complete loss as to what to do or which way to turn.

He had spent all his life ignoring his father's advice that he should let things be and clung on to his unreasonable hatred of him, his certainty that his father was the wrongdoer and that he didn't want his son to stumble upon the truth. How wrong he had been, and as a result so many important years had been tragically wasted. It was only right, he had supposed, that he should be made to see his mother for what she was, shallow yet devious, a user yet used, avaricious and totally unprincipled, incapable of giving or receiving love or any worthwhile emotion, sunk in vice and corruption and wallowing in wealth amassed by her own cunning, bought with her own soul.

Quila had been sickened to the depths of his being, but had remained with her until he had been no longer able to bear it. He wrote a stilted letter of apology to his father, who had responded immediately, asking him to come back and take over the farm. But he had felt he could not, and that he could never lay claim to anything that belonged to the father he had spent his life rejecting. Far better that his half-brother be looked upon as the heir. So Quila had remained in America, working and roaming from one place to another, until his last employer, a large landowner, recognised and greatly valued his skills. Only recently had he decided to return to the land of his birth.

Romy greeted her parents warmly and over afternoon tea, she related the events of the past week, omitting all mention of Quila. She learned that Leon had been working hard in her absence and had the tennis court restored to its original condition and had begun scything the long grass in the orchard. Romy was happy to hear of his progess but was contrary in her hope that Leon didn't work too quickly in future, as she felt she was going to need a lot with which to occupy her in the time ahead.

Within the privacy of her bedroom, she unpacked her suitcase and disposed of her laundry in the cane receptacle that stood in the corner of her room, then sat down on the edge of her bed and began to wonder what difference being in possession of the facts was going to make to the situation that now existed between her and Quila. 'Possibly none,' she uttered aloud. In fact she was decidedly apprehensive about meeting up with him again and found herself entertaining two conflicting desires, one to see him again and as soon as possible, while at the same time wanting only to postpone indefinitely the event of their next meeting.

As for Julie . . .

At that moment the door to her room opened and she turned to find the very subject of her thoughts entering her room. Julie closed the door with a subdued click. Yet the expression on her face was far from subdued, ominous in its pale, tight-lipped severity.

'Hello, Julie. You're home early.' Romy wanted to rise to her feet and retreat from the menacing picture her sister presented and turn away from the unpleasant glitter in her dark eyes, but found she couldn't. It was almost as if she were glued to the spot where she sat.

Julie didn't return the greeting, ignored in fact all preliminaries, and launched straight into an attack. 'Did you have a nice week away in Wellington with Quila?' she asked. And the calm with which she spoke was so at variance with the attitude of her that Romy felt alarm spring up from the very pit of her stomach.

She controlled it with difficulty and forced herself to respond equably: 'I had a lovely week.'

'With Quila.'

'I saw Quila, yes. But he and I don't exactly hit it off—as you well know.'

Julie's lips curled, marring her attractive features. 'Quila mightn't hit it off with you, but I know you of old, Romy, and I can tell that you would certainly like to hit it off with him.'

'So you have nothing to worry about, because if you do know me as well as you claim to, you should also realise that any one-sided relationship would hold no attraction for me.'

'Oh, so smug!' Julie's eyes flashed malevolence, but her voice was soft and low. 'As always. So sure of yourself, aren't you? Well, not this time. Quila won't fall under your spell, I'll see to that. This time I intend to fight for what I want. And I want Quila and I mean to have him!'

Romy shivered. There was a look of almost maniacal

hatred in Julie's eyes. Something within her cried out in protest at this unnatural emotion harboured for her by her own sister. 'Oh, Lee . . .'

'Shut up!' Julie hissed. 'Shut up and listen to me—though I know it's not easy for you to listen to me when it's always been you who's held the floor.' She paused, and Romy remained silent, aghast at the procession of expressions flitting over Julie's face, twisting it.

My God, Romy thought, she's obsessed! Obsessed with Quila, but most of all obsessed with her hatred of me. How many years, fruitless years, had she been filled with this cankerous hatred that serves only to poison both mind and body?

'Do you know what I'd like to do?' Julie drawled, though there was no relaxation of her stance or overall manner. 'I'd like to take a pair of scissors to that award-winning face of yours and cut it to ribbons!' The relish she was afforded at the mere imagining of such a horrendous action was mirrored openly in her face. Seeing it, Romy thought she would be ill. She wanted to turn away, but fascination had her caught firmly in its snare. 'But I don't think I'll have to go to such lengths, though it would give me enormous pleasure. No—I have some information, sweet sister, that would make you want only one thing—to die! Keep away from Quila or so help me, I'll make you wish, as I do, that you'd never been born. And I mean every word!' she added, and her low voice shook with conviction.

It was difficult for Romy to treat the content of her sister's threats seriously, but nonetheless Julie's behaviour could by no means be taken lightly. Was it possible that Julie could be unbalanced? Whenever she recalled the scene or dwelt on the words that had passed her sister's lips, Romy felt a chill creep over her skin and her stomach would churn nauseously until she threw herself into whatever task was in hand and temporary forgetfulness.

She never sought out Quila and neither did he attempt to establish any contact with her, and he had, since their respective visits to Wellington, stopped coming for a midday meal on Sundays. With Christmas fast approaching there was a great deal to be done and, thankful for it, Romy worked each day until she was sure she could drop into bed and oblivion. Valiantly, she kept up a cheerful disposition for her parents' sake, and for Leon's as well, because he worked so conscientiously beside her; also she didn't want the true picture of how she actually felt being conveyed, however innocently, back to Quila.

Quila. How she ached to see him! To touch him, her fingers along his forearm, her lips to his strong warm throat. How easy it was to hate him during the day and yet long for him at night. How easy it had been, it seemed, for him to forget her. What was she to do? She didn't want to leave Summerhaze, or her parents, after so short a time. Only three months. But one thing was certain, she couldn't go on existing like this— acting as though nothing was wrong between Julie and her and as though Quila meant nothing to her and his indifference towards her wasn't killing her inch by inch.

After New Year, she would leave, she decided finally; make out that the city and its bright lights were calling her. It was what everyone was expecting anyway, particularly Quila. Well, let him think he was right about her. What did it matter when he wanted only to be proved right, nothing else, and certainly not her. But first, before she went, she would organise a grand New Year's Eve party, a replica of those they had once held at Summerhaze up at the woolshed every New Year's Eve without fail. She'd invite all their friends and relatives and neighbours. She would plan and finance it, and it would be her great farewell gesture and one which she intended to enjoy to the fullest.

But first there was Christmas to get through when, as was customary, they would stop off at Nellie's, pick her up and take her along to church and bring her back to have Christmas dinner with them at Summerhaze. As it turned out, Nellie was not to be the only guest that Christmas Day, for Romy soon learned that Quila and Leon had been invited to the homestead for the festive meal as well, and she had to come to grips with the prospect of having to face Quila for the first time in nearly six weeks. Feeling as she did, she knew it was not going to be easy, and an even greater ordeal was going to be the endless afternoon that proceeded the meal.

Little did she know, however, that her problems were to begin a lot earlier than that. The moment she opened her eyes on Christmas morning, her first instinct was to recoil in both shock and disbelief at the sight that greeted her. She hoisted herself into a sitting position and, in the grip of timeless stupefaction, gazed at the hank of plaited blonde hair that lay across her pillow. It lay there! was all that her incredulous mind could assimilate. While ... Her hand flew to her head—while the other still remained intact on the right side of her head. Closing her eyes, she gingerly, and in dread, explored the left side of her head and gagged as her fingertips encountered a stump of uneven, bristly, newly cut hair. Her stomach heaved and she leapt off her bed and made it in time to the ornamental porcelain water jug and bowl set resting on the top of her chest of drawers.

Some indeterminable time later, she felt sufficiently composed to leave the bowl and hovered in the vicinity of the cheval mirror. She sank down on a stool before it, and immediately her eyes streamed with tears and she cried as weakly and unashamedly as a baby.

How much time elapsed before she pulled herself together and felt adequately competent to take a pair of scissors to her other plait, she didn't know. If her head had actually been shaved clean, she couldn't have felt more dreadful than she did at that moment, staring with a fixity at the two stubs of blunt cut hair reaching only to the middle of her ears.

Quila was coming to dinner today, she realised bleakly, and this—this was Julie's handiwork, a warning. Julie had come into her room some time during the night—with a pair of scissors! Again Romy's stomach lurched with revulsion. She fought back the tide of nausea and sat and waited until the fit of shivering had abated. Then, with deceptive calm, she rose, searched for and found a suitable scarf and, with fingers that shook, tied it over her head. What was she going to do with such a mess? This being Christmas Day, there was nothing she could do, she concluded at length, except try to make the best of the situation. Who would question her wearing a scarf to church—or even to the table, as the meal was going to be enjoyed out of doors.

As she caught sight of her wan face and tragic expression, tears welled up again, but after only a few moments she came to accept the futility of self-pity and resolved to do the only thing there was left to do in the circumstances, clean up and present herself looking as stunning and as dramatic as possible. Thus, contrary to her original intention to appear as inconspicuous as she could, she descended the stairs, dressed for church in a summer creation of swirling silk, striped in exotic hues of plum and green, with one of the two stripes of black shot through with gold thread. She chose plum-coloured accessories and gold jewellery, among which were large hooped ear-rings at her ears, and every strand of hair was out of sight beneath a dexterously tied scarf of corresponding plum. Her make-up was dramatic, without being overdone, and although her smattering of freckles was adroitly concealed, she endeavoured to enhance her tan as much as possible, at the same time ensuring that her eyes and mouth were, at first glance, startling in contrast. Perfect, she had thought with no sense of satisfaction whatsoever. Far from achieving her objective, Julie's action was going to succeed only in pushing her despised sister into the forefront of attention, something which neither of them wanted.

As it happened, Romy was to be more thankful and rely more heavily on the support of her appearance than she could have ever foreseen. It wasn't easy for her to behave with normality in the presence of Quila when the scene of their last time together had ever since occupied a place of prominence in her thoughts. And to make it especially difficult was the awareness of Julie's ever watchful eye on her, both triumphant yet wary, and the recollection of her own horrifying discovery upon waking that morning playing over and over in her mind. She ate little and, when not making a pretence at joviality, remained expressionless, enigmatic behind her mask, so that if her eyes should betray her by straying in Quila's direction, they would give nothing away.

The meal was comprised of traditional dishes, roast

lamb, buttered and minted new potatoes and green peas, plus a variety of salads, followed by Christmas pudding and brandy sauce, or trifle and fresh fruit salad for those who preferred to be less traditional in view of the hot weather.

Romy was only too glad to assign herself to the task of transferring the soiled dishes back inside to the kitchen, and when Quila made it obvious that he intended to assist, she protested, telling him she could manage with Leon's help.

'I don't want Leon turning into your lapdog,' he told her, keeping pace with her as she strode away in the direction of the side entrance to the house.

Romy bridled. Once in the kitchen she dumped the dishes down on the wooden table with a clatter and turned to glare at Quila. 'You're a swine!' she railed at him, finding it almost impossible to maintain her grip on her temper made precariously fragile not only by Quila's snide remarks but by the event that had begun the day. 'Leon and I are friends, and whether your warped mind can contend with that or not, it's the truth. Now get out and leave me to deal with these on my own.'

'Mmm, frayed temper and sullen disposition,' he drawled, resting his hands on the back of his hips, arrogant and yet so attractive in his beige slacks and brick red open-necked shirt that Romy's heart quickened in spite of herself. 'I see that life in the country is beginning to pall. Who are you trying to remind that you're a number one glamour queen, all decked up like a Christmas package?'

'You, maybe,' she riposted.

'I don't need reminding, believe me.'

'Then maybe I need to remind myself!' she flashed recklessly. 'That life is not all flies and dirt under the fingernails, gumboots and oilskins and people reeking of sweat and cow manure. I know only too well how you disapprove of the way I live my life, but thank God I don't need your approval before I take each breath!'

There was silence, during which brown eyes clashed with a silver-green pair that sparkled brilliantly between blackened lashes and coloured lids.

'So when do you leave?' asked Quila.

'I'm going to leave, am I?'

'I imagine so.'

'You mean you hope so! You'd just hate to be proved wrong, wouldn't you? You wouldn't admit it even if you were, would you?' She sighed. 'Very well, I'll not disappoint you.' And with that she brushed past him into the sunshine which struck her so brightly, so fiercely, her eyes watered under the attack.

That evening, when finally alone in her room, she sat once again before her mirror and slowly untied her scarf and tried not to wince at the sight of her hacked hair but to retain the stoicism she had built up during the course of the day. There seemed nothing for it but to wash it and attempt to cut it herself until it bore some semblance of a style. Then first thing following Boxing Day she would go into Masterton and seek out a hairdresser game enough to rectify the damage.

CHAPTER NINE

DURING the week that followed, Romy and Leon worked long and hard to prepare the woolshed for the New Year's Eve party. It was swept and washed until it was as clean as it was possible to make it, and then decorated with lanterns and balloons, and streamers, cut, blended and twisted by their own hands. The piano was transported from the house and installed in one corner, and the trestles used for the children's picnic and lunch on Christmas Day were yet again assembled and covered with the scarlet linen that had been laundered after its use on Christmas Day.

Romy's time was taken up completely with these tasks as well as the planning of the menu, the hiring of glasses and crockery and ordering drinks and the additional food which she knew that neither she nor her mother were going to be able to prepare themselves.

There was going to be no dance band as such, since her father could play the fiddle superbly and volunteered his services, also many of their invited guests could play the piano, guitar, banjo and piano accordion and had offered to bring along instruments that weren't available and keep the party swinging.

By the time New Year's Eve arrived, Romy was feeling positively exuberant and caught up in the mood of the festivities that were about to begin. She was one hundred per cent satisfied with all the arrangements and equally certain that the evening was going to be a grand success.

She dressed in a full, gaily patterned skirt and

wedge-heeled sandals, and her dainty white blouse, with its covered buttons and delicate white embroidered pattern, left her arms bare and the deeply scooped neckline revealed an expanse of honeyed skin. After applying moisturiser to her skin and the minimum of make-up, she sat back and studied her reflection in her mirror.

How long and slender her neck looked, she thought, now that her hair was short. Vulnerable and exposed— as she herself felt these days. Hastily she rejected the thought. Since Christmas Day, she hadn't allowed herself time to dwell on her feelings and it would be folly to begin an investigation now. Nevertheless, she sat where she was for a moment or two longer and wondered how Quila would see her tonight. Looking as she did now, with her hair short, curling softly about her face, the sharp planes and angles of which had softened over the preceding few months and the once pale skin now tanned and blooming with good health, she thought the only advertisement hoarding she could possibly feature in was one promoting New Zealand apples. She gave a grimace of rueful satisfaction. She needed to obliterate from Quila's mind the picture she had presented on Christmas Day and try to eradicate from his memory the impression she had, under stress, deliberately and rashly given him that she intended to return to the way of life she had previously assured him that she had renounced.

Tonight, she vowed to herself, it was all or nothing. If Quila persisted in treating her as though she were a member of another and altogether repugnant species, then she would have no alternative but to admit defeat and plan a life for herself away from her beloved home and put between them a distance of hundreds of miles. Then the field would be clear for Julie, but in the meantime she had decided she wasn't going to succumb to intimidation or acts of barbarism. She too was going to put up a fight for the only man she had ever wanted and to whom she was capable of giving far more than her sister ever could. ·

But as the evening progressed, she was forced to accept the futility of her hopes and her heart which, at first so high and buoyant with optimism, began its long painful descent. Although she caught his dark gaze on her on several occasions, she could read nothing into his expression, and he made no attempt at all to approach to either speak to her or to ask her to dance. Not even one dance. And to compound her despair still further, she watched him take Julie into his arms for the last sequence before midnight.

All at once the heat within the woolshed became unendurable and the smell of food, mingling with a range of other indeterminable odours, began to sicken her. As unobtrusively as she could, she slipped away and once down the numerous steps extending from the woolshed to the ground, she began running until she was eventually swallowed up in a honeysuckle-perfumed darkness where the silence was broken only by the cicadas. It was then that she slackened her pace but kept on walking nonetheless, beyond the homestead and garden towards the bay.

The night was clear and warm, with a stiff cooling breeze coming in off the moonlit sea. But the breeze wasn't enough to cool Romy, even hotter now after her exertion, and the walk itself hadn't been exercise enough to shake off the demon of torment to prevent it from winding its poisonous strangling tentacles about her heart. Kicking off her sandals and divesting herself of her skirt and blouse, she ran, clad only in her bikini briefs, into the gently buffeting surf, submerging and surfacing only to submerge again, as if by repeating the ritual she could purge her mind as well as her body. The farther out she swam the colder the water became, reminding her to keep her head and not stray too far from shore.

How long she had been in before she became aware of a very chilling certainty that she wasn't alone, she couldn't tell. Her heart seemed to stop dead within her. Was it Julie? Was she deranged enough to try to drown her? Panicking, she struck out for shore and experienced an overwhelming sense of relief when a wave, stronger than most, propelled her forward until she felt the rasp of sand against her breasts and thighs. Pulling herself upright, she ran as fast as she could towards the small mound of clothes revealed in the moonlight as being almost caught by the incoming tide. But the strength had seemed to have gone from her limbs, sapped by her rigorous swim and, her steps impeded still further by the wet heavy sands, she fell on to her knees in the shallow, effervescent surf.

Turning frantically, she saw, not Julie, but the figure of a man coming up behind her, and her heart lurched laboriously. 'Who—who is it?' Her demand was ejected from between her lips not in a formidable voice but one quivering with ill-concealed fear.

'It's Quila,' came the reply, after what seemed an eternity.

Reaction set in immediately and her knees began to tremble so violently, she doubted that they would support her, but even so she had to try to get to her feet. 'What are you doing here? Did you follow me? And don't come any closer!' A shrill note entered her voice as she glanced over her shoulder and saw him drawing nearer. 'Can't you see I'm not dressed properly?'

'I can see,' he replied after some delay. 'But what I

can't see is what difference it makes. You're very rarely dressed "properly".'

'That's your opinion!' she retorted vexedly, and reaching her clothes, she pulled on her blouse and fastened the buttons over her still wet breasts. She turned to face him. 'Besides, you're also in your underwear, so you can't talk.'

'But adequately covered.'

'If I'd known I was going to be honoured with your illustrious company,' she came close to sneering, 'I'd have made sure that I too was adequately covered. What are you doing here anyway?'

'I wanted to wish you a happy New Year.'

'So you did follow me?'

'I suppose I must have,' he conceded mildly, stepping closer and reaching for her.

Her nerves jumped, pumping through her system the adrenaline required to enable her to sidestep him. 'Don't you dare touch me! Isn't Julie enough for you?'

He emitted a soft, slightly self-deprecating laugh. 'Julie is a beautiful woman, but she doesn't kiss the way you do.'

'That's too bad, isn't it?' In spite of her bravado and her responses delivered in a hard quelling voice, Romy had to acknowledge that he was unnerving her in a way that she had never been before, and her stomach muscles started to knot with fear. A quick glance confirmed that his bulk was now fixed firmly between herself and her skirt, which had been caught by the tide and was bobbing on the surface of the water. She forced herself not to give in to her desire to retreat several steps away from him.

'But most importantly, I don't see the promise in her eyes that I see in yours.'

She did back away then. 'What . . .?' she quailed. 'What on earth are you talking about . . .?'

'You know only too well what I'm talking about.' Quila reached for her and this time there was no evading him or obstructing his purpose. 'I might not have had much experience with women of your sort, but I know when a woman wants a man and I, fool that I am, want you like hell.' His laughter seemed to come from deep within his throat, mocking himself as much, if not more than her. 'There must be more of my father in me that I realised,' he got out between closed teeth, sealing her quivering, struggling body tightly against the length of his, 'when I'm so tempted to take whatever's offering, especially when knowing full well that what I'm being offered is trash.'

Incensed, she lashed out like a goaded animal that had been wounded and cruelly tormented beyond its endurance. As she wrestled with him, she felt the fine, very beautiful fabric of her blouse rip and was maddened even further, and her rage gave her the strength she needed to free her arms and bring up her fists to batter them against his ears. Then, quite suddenly, she was free. She stumbled back in surprise and almost fell. Recovering her balance, she glowered at him, half his face clearly visible in the light of the moon, the other half concealed by shadows.

'You—*animal*!' she expostulated, and cried out in protest and frustration as once again he caught her and held her fast against the hard, wet, near-naked length of him. She suffered the wrench of her arms being yanked behind her and both wrists secured easily by one of his hands. Twisting her head aside, she vowed that she would fight until she dropped with exhaustion before she allowed his lips to touch hers.

Contrary to her expectations, however, he made no

attempt to kiss her mouth, instead she felt the soft gliding of his lips across her exposed shoulder and the almost tantalising rasp of his shaven skin against hers. Smothering a gasp, she stiffened and tried to jerk free of the searing seduction of his mouth, but she might just as well have been expecting steel to yield to her puny strength. The hand had been exploring and caressing the curve of her hip, closed on her, straining her closer while his mouth moved insidiously up over her neck, pressing against the more sensitive areas until reaching the pulsating hollow just below her ear where he allowed it to rest. Her senses were swimming and she knew that like his, her body was throbbing and her breath was coming much too quickly. She *had* to resist him.

'Let me go, Quila.' She had managed to prevent herself from pleading with him and was relieved—however, there was nothing she could have done about the husky cracked quality of her voice.

His hold on her relaxed a fraction. 'Are you sure you want me to let you go?' he whispered against her ear, allowing his hand to trail upward over her stomach.

She shuddered, jerking to try and escape his touch. 'Let me go!'

This time Quila didn't prevaricate. Abruptly his arms fell to his sides and she was free.

Her relief was so tremendous, it gave vent to an anger of which she scarcely knew she was capable. She brought her hand up and across his face with every ounce of strength she had left. '*Don't* you ever touch me again!' She sidestepped him, paused to scoop up her wet sandals and skirt, then turned and on quaking limbs strode up over the sand to the road.

Belatedly it occurred to her that had he wanted to,

he could have avoided the blow she had dealt him, for her arm, which had responded to her will, had been trembling and as weighty as lead. Why he hadn't ducked, she told herself, she neither knew nor cared, and she refused to dwell on her action or feel any sense of compunction whatsoever.

If only she had had the strength to give him what he truly deserved, she thought, gritting her teeth and fiercely swallowing back the tears welling up within her.

In an attempt to blot out what had just taken place, she began to run along the road's grassy verge. At times she cut her bare feet on the occasional sharp-edged stones which had been spat up by passing traffic, but nevertheless she didn't stop until she had reached the sanctuary of the tree-shrouded gates of Summerhaze. Once there, she fell against the trunk of the enormous sycamore, gasping painfully, positive that at any minute her lungs would burst.

When at last she considered herself to be as composed as she was ever likely to be, she pushed herself upright and began fumbling with her skirt. Wringing it out first, she then pulled it down over her head and zipped it up. She fastened the remaining buttons on her ruined blouse, slipped her feet into her uncomfortably wet sandals and made her way through the trees towards the house, praying inwardly that everyone would still be up at the woolshed and too busy enjoying themselves to notice her absence.

However, had she been the only absent one then she might have been fortunate, but it was Quila's absence that was bound to be noticed by at least one of the guests, and dismay flooded through her as she saw Julie only too clearly in her red dress, standing on the verandah, watching and waiting for her as she came through the trees and up the sloping lawn to the verandah steps.

There was venom in her unblinking glare, rage and hatred in every line of her body and every muscle in her taut white face. After one glance, Romy couldn't bear to look at her. With a dreadful nausea gathering in the pit of her stomach, she climbed the steps, and eventually drew level with her sister.

'*You!*' she snapped. 'You—alleycat!'

If Romy had had the courage to look at her, she would have seen Julie's arm rise and might have been able to duck and avoid the blow which, as it was, struck her full across the face, just below her nose, and sent her reeling down three of the seven steps she had just climbed and crashing into the handrail which she flung her hands out to catch and cling to for support while the world went into a pain-filled, light-studded spin.

When everything finally stabilised once more, she opened her eyes, which were smarting with tears, and put her hand up gingerly to her mouth, the top lip of which was numb and felt twice its size. Incredulously, she lifted her head and gazed up at her sister who, with fists clenched, looked not only unrepentant but fully prepared to repeat her performance.

'Look at you!' she snarled. 'Just look at yourself!'

'Julie . . .'

'Shut up! *Shut up!*' Her voice had sharpened to a shrillness which gave birth to a fear in Romy, not only of Julie but for her.

As she righted herself, Romy's hesitation was barely perceptible before she sprang up the steps, passed Julie and through the front door into the house. She made it to the stairs and had just embarked up them when Julie apprehended her yet again.

'Don't run away from me yet. I haven't finished

what I've got to say to you—not by a long chalk. When I've said all I intend to, then you can run—and when you've heard what I've got to say, I'm sure that even the distance between here and New York won't be great enough!'

Faint with fatigue that was both mental and physical, Romy stood quite still, facing away from her sister and maintaining a firm grip on the banister.

'Whatever Romy wanted, Romy took,' was grated out behind her. 'And it was always the same. You did nothing but take. Right from the very beginning you usurped me, taking over first place in my parents' affections, inveigling your way into the place of priority in our home and in our lives, taking over my boyfriends, constantly pushing me out as though I didn't belong, when all along it was you who didn't belong.'

Quite sure now that her sister was demented, Romy began to shake with the strain of not knowing what to do, whether to stay where she was and try to reason with her, or walk on up to her room without uttering a word.

'Look at me, Romy!' the command rang out harshly. 'Turn around and look at me!' Romy felt her arm taken, gripped as though in a vice, and she was swung about as easily as if she'd been no bigger or heavier than an eight-year-old child. 'Now it's my turn to *take*—the pleasure of seeing your face when I tell you a few home truths about a few things around here, dear sweet sister of mine. Truths that should have been used to slap you down a good many years before now!'

'Julie, don't you think that this has gone far enough?' Romy pleaded, trying desperately to introduce a thread of sanity into this bizarre situation. 'I never took anything that belonged to you . . .'

'You took my parents' affection away from me!' Julie

exploded, bringing her hand down with a resounding crack on the banister. 'You took over *my* place in *my* family!'

'What *are* you talking about? This is *my* family too. Just as much mine as it is yours.'

'*No!*'

'No,' Julie repeated a fraction more calmly. 'That's where you're wrong, where you've always been wrong. This is nobody's family but *mine*! You don't belong here, Romy, with us at Summerhaze. You never did. You were a stray, a nobody, picked up by Mr and Mrs Matthew Palliser. Your true father wasn't known and your mother was a tramp. She didn't want you. She cast you off and abandoned you.'

'My God, you *are* mad!' Romy gasped.

'No. Oh, no, indeed I'm not. In fact if I'd been as sane as I am now, I would have told you your true position years ago. You were adopted,' she almost spat the word, 'and were always given the best of everything and always more than me because of my parents' misguided idea that life had in some way deprived you. Huh!' Julie snorted scornfully. 'Your sort are never deprived. What they want they just *take* . . . Stay where you are!' she ordered as Romy turned dazedly away.

To Romy the entire situation had become too fantastic to be real. It was as though the two of them were the principal characters acting out their respective roles in some kind of black comedy, while all around the air kept getting darker and more oppressive, closing in on her until she felt certain that if she didn't escape she would be overcome, smothered. But in spite of the impending threat, she found herself responding to her sister's wishes like a robot under remote control.

'I haven't finished yet,' Julie was saying, 'and I've saved the best till last. Look at me, Romy.'

Unable to defy her, and not even knowing if she wanted to any longer, Romy looked back over her shoulder, repelled and yet fascinated by this side to her sister she had never before seen or known existed.

'Quila Morgan is not Summerhaze's manager. He never was. Only someone as egotistical as you would have ever believed that he was. While you were off travelling in distant lands, basking in fame and fortune, the father you professed to love so much was catapulting headlong into bankruptcy. He was grief-stricken when Uncle Bob was killed and then, as if that wasn't enough, he had to contend with the colossal disappointment of Sean and Kit wanting to sell out. He mortgaged Summerhaze and bought them out, but his health had been failing even then and he was unable to bear up under the strain and financial burdens that were too great to incur at his time of life. It had almost been too late when Quila Morgan came along—but not quite. With his tidy bank balance, he saved the day.'

'What . . .' Romy had to clear her throat, she felt as though a hand had gripped her there and was slowly squeezing it closed. 'What are you trying to say?'

'Haven't you figured it out?' Julie taunted.

'Quila doesn't own Summerhaze. He can't do. The idea is preposterous!'

'Not quite so preposterous. He and Dad are partners. One day, Dad will sell out to him in toto—that's understood.'

'You're lying! About this as you've lied about everything!'

'Check it out,' Julie suggested with a flippancy that was engendered by her assurance of victory. 'It's true enough, but check it out with Quila, or Dad, if you must—if you dare.'

Romy felt her knees buckle and she leaned weakly

against the banister, a hand lifting to press against temples now throbbing so violently she thought her head would explode.

'Well, well,' Julie was gloating softly. 'How long I've waited for this day! To see Miss High and Mighty come down off her mountain, brought down to the level of her "inferiors" and made to breathe the less refined air!' She laughed unpleasantly. 'How does it feel,' she mocked, 'to realise how Quila must have been laughing up his sleeve at you all these months? Ordering him about—as though *you* were the boss's daughter and he was the hired hand, when neither was true.'

With a tremendous effort, Romy made her knees straighten and support her body without the aid of the banister rail. She looked into her sister's face and saw her brown eyes a glitter and her face flushed with the pleasure she had so obviously been afforded by the role she had finally been given the opportunity to play. 'I'm—I'm sorry for whatever it is I've done in the past that's made you feel this way about me—hate me to this extent. I pity you . . .'

'Don't waste your energy pitying me!' Julie flared. 'Save it for yourself.'

Romy's lips twisted in a wry grimace. 'I won't need it. After being given the opportunity to see first-hand the results of it, I most assuredly won't be availing myself of it.'

Julie's smile was one of icy disdain. She tossed her head. 'All's fair in love and war—it was *you* who taught me that, and for the first time, I've won a round!'

'Is that what you'd call it? Well, if it's what you wanted so badly for so long and you now have it at last, I'm pleased for you.' Indescribably weary, her face, her head, almost every part of her body throbbing with pain, Romy turned and climbed the stairs. On leadened legs it seemed a long way to the top and she was almost glad of the reprieve ordered by Julie's question:

'When will you be leaving?'

'Don't worry, I'll try not to waste any time.'

'What will you tell Mum and Dad?'

Although the questions were asked in an aggressive tone, Romy detected the underlining of anxiety in the second one and this brought her around to look down directly into her sister's face. 'Nothing of what has passed between us tonight. Any confession or explanation they'll get will have to come from you, Julie. Sleep on that.'

CHAPTER TEN

Six months had passed since that fateful night when Romy had lain in her bed, stricken and sleepless. While outwardly calm, inwardly she had quivered and trembled all through, unable to pinpoint exactly what was trembling and helpless to quell or even control it.

How strange it had all been! In her heart she had felt so cold, so numb. If only she could *feel* something, she had thought almost desultorily. Hatred, anger, grief—anything, but not this—nothingness. Oh, God, why was it all so easy to believe, so easy to accept? By rights she should be doing battle with great tides of sheer incredulity, disbelief.

But she never did. Instead there had been times when she could have almost sworn she was glad. Glad that it was finally over, all these endless wearying wasted years of wondering at the full reason behind Julie's fanatical jealousy and resentment of her. At last she knew, and knowledge had brought a strange sense of release, relief too, as it had suddenly become clear to her that even if she had known right from the beginning, she would have been absolutely powerless to change the circumstances of her being who she was and where she was.

Two days following her revelations, Julie had announced that she had decided to go to visit a school friend who was married and living up north and always issuing her with invitations to stay with them. Romy had known that her sister had fully expected her to be gone by the time she arrived back. And, of course,

Julie had her wish. How could Romy possibly have stayed on and lived as though she were still in ignorance of the truth surrounding her origins and the facts lurking behind Quila's presence at Summerhaze?

As weeks turned into months, Romy often wondered if there might be something vitally amiss with her, in that after the initial shock and subsequent analysis, she was able to accept and dismiss the fact that she had been adopted as a baby and that there was no flesh and blood link between her and the man and woman she had, all her life, looked upon as her parents, almost with detachment and a total lack of emotion. Whereas the realisation that her father—and she knew she could never think of him as being anything else—kept from her the facts pertaining to Quila had wounded her too deeply for words. He had lied to her, and by withholding the truth from her, he had shut her out. As though she didn't really belong at all and that Julie had been right, she never had! Yes, that always cut through her afresh whenever she allowed her mind to dwell on it.

And even though her mother had flown to Auckland to visit her three months earlier, to explain that Julie had suffered a breakdown and had confessed to the enormity of what she had done, and even though she could accept and understand her mother's explanation as to why her father had deceived her as he had, she knew she could never go back.

Her father was a proud man and he loved her, and knew only too well how much she cared for Summerhaze. Of course he wanted to save her for as long as he could from the knowledge that Summerhaze was now partly owned by a stranger. He had thought that once she had got to know, like and respect Quila, she would be happy about the decision he had made.

And as her mother had explained, even if her father had accepted her financial help, the time would have come and would have had to be faced when Summerhaze would have to be sold and they would have had to move into the city or retire up North as had many farmers who had no sons to take over from them.

Privately, Romy didn't agree with her mother on this. In her heart she was sure she could have taken over Summerhaze, hired a good manager and remained on her home until the end of her days. Not that it was much use speculating on that possibility now. It was too late. She knew she would never, could never go back to stay. Not ever. According to Nina, Quila was under the impression that she had tired of Summerhaze and had since resumed her modelling career. And while inwardly she had been rent with pain, outwardly she had been careful to betray to her mother nothing of what she was feeling. Let him think what he liked, she had thought bitterly, and had remarked carelessly to her mother that it certainly was an idea and one which she would consider.

As her mother was leaving, Romy had promised that she would make a visit down to the Wairarapa before long, but three months had slipped by and, although anxious not to cause her father more sorrow than she knew he had already suffered, she was loath to be in any locality where the danger of bumping into Quila became distinctly real.

As for Julie, Romy harboured no ill feeling towards her, nor withheld her forgiveness, and wrote to her at least once a month, although she never received nor expected any reply.

The apartment she had found for herself in Auckland was situated in the popular suburb of Takapuna, now a city in its own right. It was modern, attractive and located only a matter of five minutes' walk from the sea and, because it was an upstairs flat, Romy was able to see the glittering blue Pacific from her lounge and bedroom windows.

Takapuna itself quite appealed to Romy, but the city as a whole she abhorred. After having lived in cities such as London and Paris, and even New York, she found it in comparison a disaster. A sprawling mess, with an abysmal lack of planning and character, but with its full quota of other big city disadvantages such as noise and countless thoroughfares of polluting traffic. And the heat! She could take the clear dry heat of the east coast any time, but not this appalling humidity. How she longed to go home. *Damn* Quila Morgan!

Each morning, as she walked into Takapuna and to the publishing house where she had found a job as a receptionist, she uttered the same curse, and her heart wrung. Would she ever forget him? And whatever could she do to hasten the process?

Winter arrived, bringing a freshness to the air that Romy welcomed, and it must have improved her temper and outlook, for she began to find herself having attention lavished on her at her place of work by certain males who had been initially inclined to keep their distance.

She fended them off without expending too much effort, for her sense of humour was at last beginning to be restored. In the end, however, she found herself mellowing towards one young man, Grant Johnson, shyer than the rest, who didn't smother her with his presence or pay her fulsome compliments, and when he asked her out it was done in a discreet fashion that elevated him in her estimation. He was nice, she considered. There was something honest and wholesome about him. If she turned him down, she suspected he would honour her decision and not ask her again. So she accepted his invitation to dine and found to her surprise that she enjoyed his company enormously. He took her to a restaurant which, although unremarkable in appearance, served exceptionally good food, and kept her entertained with his easy conversation and ready, rather dry wit.

Perhaps, she thought as she bade him goodnight at her door, the process had begun. At last she was on the road to putting Quila Morgan behind her. She wandered across to the window of the lounge and stood in the darkness staring out over the rooftops of houses that stood amidst gardens, trees and shrubs between her flat and the black still waters of the bay.

Suddenly the telephone rang, shattering the silence and causing her to start right out of her new found sense of peace and wellbeing. Who on earth would be ringing her at this hour? A picture of her father flashed unbidden into her mind and dread turned her cold. She made a quick dash to the telephone and got out her greeting and number in a breathless rush.

'Romy? It's Quila.'

At the sound of his voice, Romy felt peculiarly lightheaded and her heart had to beat at twice its normal rate to pump back the blood which seemed to have drained from her head.

'Romy?'

'I'm—still here.' She swallowed hard, aware of the strange ticking of her pulse at her throat. 'It's Pop, isn't it? Something's happened to him?'

'No, of course not. Everyone's fine.'

The onslaught of relief, though overwhelming, was swift to turn to anger. 'What do you mean, "of course not"? Do you realise you're ringing me at one in the morning?'

'Only because I knew I wouldn't be able to get you before. Your friendly next-door neighbour told me you went out looking dressed to kill with a very personable escort.'

'How—how could you possibly be speaking to my neighbour?'

'I saw her earlier this evening. She passed me as I was just about to knock on your door.'

Romy felt for and found a stool and sat down heavily upon it. 'You're in Auckland?' she asked in a voice too highly pitched.

'Yes.'

'Why?'

'To see you.' His voice sounded deep and sincere, but although Romy noted its quality, she promptly dismissed it as having no relevance.

'Well, I'm sorry if you came all this way simply to see me, which I doubt, because I really have no desire to see you.'

'I won't believe that, Romy,' he came back unequivocally. 'I know I hurt you . . .'

'You didn't,' she cut in.

'And you hurt me—constantly.'

Romy struggled to maintain her grip on her sense of reality, which seemed to be slipping inexorably away from her. Hoping she sounded more phlegmatic than she felt, she demanded: 'How can someone you despise possibly have the power to hurt you?—did my parents put you up to coming up here to try and talk me into coming home?'

'Of course they didn't. I'd have had no part in it even if they had. I'm here because I want to be here. And I want to see you. I mean to see you, Romy— tomorrow night after work. And don't try to avoid me by going out or else I'll camp down on your doorstep and remain there for a week if necessary.' So saying, he hung up.

The following day passed with Romy in rather a daze. She carried out her work mechanically and conducted her conversations in what she hoped was an intelligible manner. Grant had, much to her relief, been scheduled to visit Wellington branch that day, for to have had to chat and behave with him as though nothing untoward had taken place between their parting the night before and their meeting again that morning would most certainly have been beyond her.

She had been unable to face breakfast and had eaten scarcely at all during her lunch break, and even as she prepared a meal in her kitchen that evening, she was still too churned up to feel any real pangs of hunger. Nevertheless, after taking a shower and donning a pair of cream linen trousers and a loose-knit olive green sweater with a low V-neck and dolman sleeves she went through the motions of preparing a salad and peppering one of the two steaks she had bought in case Quila should arrive before dinner.

Which was precisely what he did, and even though she was expecting the doorbell to ring at any moment, she started violently when the rather piercing buzz sounded throughout the flat. How was she ever going to manage to appear calm and insouciant when to lay claim to a disposition of charm and sophistication seemed, for once, to be a feat quite beyond her? Her hands were shaking, she discovered, as she reached for the door knob, and she knew that because of the upheaval that had gone on within her during the course of that day, her face had lost almost every vestige of colour and whatever had been left had certainly been chased away now.

'Hello, Quila,' she greeted him, all at once determined that the poise she had spent years perfecting should not be allowed to desert her now.

'Hello, Romy.'

'Come in,' she invited, and turned away, finding it necessary to snatch momentary respite from the directness of his gaze which had lost none of the intensity she so well remembered.

She led him into the lounge, illuminated solely by the soft glow radiating from a corner lamp. She pulled the curtains and turned back to him, but still delayed the inevitable moment when she would have to meet his eyes. 'Can I take your coat? It looks as though it's been raining quite heavily.'

'It seems to have set in.' He shrugged out of his coat and Romy took it and hung it to dry off in the laundry. Upon re-entering the lounge, she indicated that he should sit down, which he did, but forward in the chair as though not feeling sufficiently at ease to relax and make himself comfortable and at home.

'Would you like a drink? I haven't much of a range, I'm afraid. Only wine or sherry.'

'Have you a beer?'

'Oh, yes, I think there's a can or two in the fridge. It was so hot and sticky in Auckland during the summer that I took a fancy to it myself.' She returned with a glass of lager for him and a sherry for herself and sat down, adopting what she hoped was a more relaxed posture than his. 'I was just about to prepare a meal before you came, though I wasn't exactly sure whether you'd invited yourself to dinner or not.'

'I haven't eaten. I would have suggested we go out to eat, but I think what we have to say to each other would be best said in private.'

'Oh?' casually. 'I really didn't think we had anything at all to say to each other.' She held her glass firmly and brought her wrist down to rest hard on her thigh so as to conceal from him the trembling of her hand.

'On the contrary,' Quila returned obliquely.

'Well, I must say you're looking well.'

And in response to this remark, his eyes made an open assessment of her face and figure. 'I'm afraid I can't say the same for you. You're looking very pale. Is something the matter?'

Romy stiffened. 'It is the middle of winter!' she flashed, allowing her own eyes to appraise his face and his body clad in grey slacks and a sweater of thick charcoal-grey wool. 'Even you bear witness to that.'

'You're looking thin, too. Like you did when you first arrived back at Summerhaze.'

'A model does have to keep her figure,' she reminded him rather acidly.

'Even an ex-model?'

She was in the process of lifting her glass to her lips when she lowered it again to ask: 'What do you mean?'

'You said you'd given it up.'

Romy's smile contained more mockery than humour. 'Since when did you take to believing anything I said?'

'I never did.'

A shaft of pain stabbed through her and she was forced to lower her eyes to her drink. 'Well,' she tried to keep the bitterness from edging her laugh, 'at least that's the truth.'

'And so is this. I wanted to, and you'll never know how much, but I didn't believe all you said because I felt I could never allow myself to.' There followed a strained silence during which their gazes met, faltered, only to meet again. 'I've come because I want to apologise for all that I've done and said to malign you.'

'Apologise?' Romy echoed with a kind of hushed incredulity. 'After all this time? Why? Why at all?'

'Some months ago I went to see Aunt Nellie,' he told her. 'She was good enough to tell me some things I didn't know.'

With an expanding sense of horror, Romy dropped her gaze and averted her head. *Surely* Nellie didn't tell him that she had guessed that Romy had once fancied herself in love with him? No—she rejected the idea utterly. Not Nellie. Dear, wise, loyal Nellie. And she relaxed and went limp and shivery with relief. 'Such as?' She leaned forward in her chair and switched on the gas fire.

'That you went to see her about me.'

'So I did,' Romy parried, bravely looking across at him once more. 'I thought there had to be something behind this obsessional hatred of me and my profession. I told you that all that was behind me, but you chose not to believe me, instead you preferred to believe that I was someone other than who I was. Somone like your mother, and it gave you a good excuse to vent out on me your hatred of her, your disgust, your opinions and your disappointments. Well, as far as I'm concerned, you made that choice deliberately. Now you've had your revenge and I have no intention of being abused by you again, nor have I any intention of apologising to you or anyone for who I am or what I've done. Is that clear?'

'As crystal.' A ghost of a self-deprecating smile came and went.

He seemed slightly at a loss and despite herself, Romy felt her heart go out to him. He dragged a hand through his wet hair and she yearned to go to him and take his head against her breast. Instead, she rose and fetched a towel and brought it to him.

'For God's sake!' he exclaimed impatiently. 'I don't need a towel.' Silently she dropped the towel on the arm of his chair and turned away. 'What I need,' he went on more quietly but just as tautly, 'desperately, is to know that you'll accept my apology and forgive me.'

'Desperately?' Romy swung around. 'A good six months have passed since I left Summerhaze, and you sit there and try to tell me that your need is desperate!'

Obviously agitated, Quila rose from the edge of his chair. 'When you left so suddenly, I wanted to know why. All your father seemed to know was that you'd felt the need to get away for a while. A month or two to sort yourself out and see what it was you wanted to do with your life. I went to see Aunt Nellie to ask her if she knew what you intended to do, if you intended to return to your career and perhaps to the U.S., but all she seemed to want to do was bait me—give me some information on which to build my hopes, and then snatched it away again just as I was about to take hold. I wrote to you. I was never one for expressing my feelings either verbally or down on paper, and it took me two solid weeks to finally manage it.'

Romy's eyes glinted with scepticism. 'And what happened to this masterpiece? *I* certainly never received it.'

'I asked Julie to post it for me. I only found out last week that she never actually posted it. While all this time I've been going through hell, waking every morning to remind myself, telling myself: "What the hell, *I* meant nothing to her, so why should my apology mean anything? She was only amusing herself with you, Quila Morgan, face up to it and forget it." After six months I can't say I've been any more successful with my self-programming than I was in the beginning. Now I want to hear you tell me one way or the other.'

During this confession, Romy had caught and held her breath, and her fascinated gaze had become ensnared in his. Did she dare believe him? 'I'm not like your mother, you know.'

'Yes, I know,' he owned quietly.

'You know—how? Because Nellie told you, no doubt?' She was powerless to prevent a hint of bitterness from creeping into her voice.

'No,' he denied. 'I think I've always known—but again I couldn't, wouldn't, allow myself to trust my inner convictions or dare to believe what I wanted to be the truth. I saw your pictures and thought it wasn't possible for anyone so lovely to want to be with only one man, to live with him away from the limelight and bear his children. I didn't dare believe it or entertain the faintest hope, so I kept reminding myself of what my mother was like.'

Romy held his gaze unflinchingly. 'No one ever made me doubt my own self-worth the way you did. Why did I let you?' she murmured, almost musingly. 'When you were wrong?'

'Will you forgive me, Romy? I need you to forgive me and I need to hear you say it.'

Their gazes locked, his dark and intense. She smiled, but not fully, for she knew she would not be able to maintain it. Nonetheless, she was coping better than he, because she could sense his consternation. 'Then of course I do. I did when Nellie told me about your mother and I first understood.' She touched his cheek lightly, intrigued as always by its matt quality, then withdrew her touch as swiftly as she had bestowed it. 'I'll go and see to dinner,' she murmured, and went quickly to the kitchen. 'How do you like your steak?' she called.

'Medium.' He had followed her and now pulled a

chair out from the table and sat down. 'It's a nice place you have here.'

'Have a look around if you like,' Romy invited, hoping that he would take her up on her offer instead of sitting there watching her every action. When he made no move, she turned once to flash a look at him and immediately felt her bones liquefy like butter that had been subjected to a fierce heat. He was staring at her with those brooding fathomless eyes but with a fixation, a hunger that had never been present before and which left her **breath**less and distinctly disorientated.

In the end the scrutiny, coupled with the silence, came too much for her to withstand. 'Why don't you— go into the lounge and put on a cassette?' she suggested, tearing the lettuce with jerky movements of her hands.

Silently he obliged her, but within seconds he was back, leaning against the door jamb, resuming his vigil—watching her.

She glanced over her shoulder and away even more swiftly, sensing him drawing her, wanting her, mesmerising her. He was not touching her and yet he was, each look as searing as an intimate caress. And although at least seven feet separated them, she could still feel his warmth enveloping her. Standing there, still and utterly silent, he seemed to be speaking volumes, wooing her, seducing her, reducing her to a tremendous *non compos mentis* mass.

'Would you—would you stop staring at me like that?' she managed at last, in querulous desperation.

'I'm sorry.' He appeared as if to make an effort to pull himself together. 'I've thought about you constantly, but dreams are a poor substitute for the real thing.'

'And if you don't mind,' she said stiltedly, 'I'd prefer you didn't speak to me like that either.'

Quila obliged her by not speaking much at all throughout the meal and they ate the steak, hot buttered potatoes and salad as though they were strangers sharing the same table in a restaurant, and Romy didn't know about Quila, but she tasted not a morsel. She felt cold all of a sudden and rose from the table to resume her place close to the gas fire in the lounge, this time sitting on a cushion which she dropped on to the floor.

Seconds later, Quila joined her, changing first the Paul Williams cassette for Rimsky-Korsakov's *Scheherazade* before coming to sit down beside her on the thick Flokati rug.

Unable to help herself, she shrank away and closer to the gas fire and rested her chin on her drawn-up knees. 'What will you do now? Go back to Summerhaze and find yourself a wife? Perhaps marry Julie?'

'No, not Julie. It was never Julie. Besides, she's now in Australia.'

Romy twisted her head to look at him, lifting her chin from her knees. 'In Australia?'

'She left last week.'

'She's recovered?'

'I think so. Once she'd made a clean breast of what she'd done, she began to make quick and steady progress. She didn't confess to me about the letter, though, until the day before she left.'

'Poor Julie! I hope she finds someone to love and who will love her in return.'

'And what about "poor Romy"? Have you found someone to love?'

She stiffened and looked away. 'Julie's needs and

my needs have always been different.'

'What about the young man who took you out last night?'

'What about him?' she shrugged carelessly. 'He's just someone I work with. Nice, but only one of many.'

'Safety in numbers, is that it?'

'I've experienced no pressing urge to find a marriage partner.'

'I thought your dream was to fill the rooms of Summerhaze with children.'

'That was when I was under a slight delusion and thought Pop was the owner of Summerhaze, lock, stock and barrel. But he isn't and never will be again. You'll own it one of these days I expect, so you'll have to fill it with children yourself. I don't belong there, and according to Julie, I never did. Perhaps she was right.'

'Have your feelings for your adoptive parents changed, then?'

'Oh, no. As if they ever could! They're my parents—my only parents, as far as I'm concerned, and I know that in their eyes, I'm as true a daughter to them as Julie is. Mum told me the story about my true parents, which Julie had distorted to some extent. Both are dead, and even if they weren't, I wouldn't want to trace them. What I meant was that my destiny doesn't lie at Summerhaze as I'd always thought it would.'

'Are you so sure about that?'

'Yes,' she reiterated flatly.

'What will you do, then?'

She shrugged. 'I have no idea. Perhaps I'll return to modelling,' she grinned at him, an impish sideways grin. 'I've got a few good years left and nothing to give it up for now.'

'What would you give it up for?' he asked. 'What would make you want to give it up for good?'

'It would have to be something really worthwhile, like a man, a home and children.'

'You'd make such a sacrifice with no regrets?'

'It would be no sacrifice. It would be like—well, like trading ashes for love, and who would object to an exchange like that?'

Suddenly she felt the touch of Quila's fingers on the exposed nape of her neck and stiffened under their gentle massaging caress. 'Why did you cut your hair, Romy?' he asked, his voice roughening slightly.

She was taken aback by the abrupt change of subject but managed to respond evenly: 'I—I suppose I wanted to see what I looked like with it short.'

'Who cut it?'

'Someone—a girl in one of the salons in Masterton.' She felt the strong fingers tighten momentarily and then move up into the fair riotous mass.

'Come to me, Romy.'

Romy remained extraordinarily still, her face rigidly averted, refusing to believe she had heard what he had said.

'Romy, look at me.'

As if in a trance, she found herself obeying the softly spoken command and the urging of his hands as they reached for her and drew her down to lie with him on the rug which was spread out before the fire.

A gasp escaped her as he brought his knee to slide up between her thighs and the lower half of his body to rest against hers, and she found her fingers curling to clutch at his woollen sweater and her eyes closing against his, unable to bear to witness the dark yet bright mingling of passion and hunger revealed there.

But in spite of the trembling of his body, and the

impassioned whispering of her name, his caress on her body was featherlight and the touch of his lips across her throat and neck, her face and features bespoke surprising restraint. She knew that her response was what he was waiting for, pleading for, as his lips played gently back and forth across her own, scarcely touching. Yet he knew, he had to know by the manner in which she clutched him and the way her knee crooked and her thigh had come to rest over his, that he could take and she would deny him nothing.

Still, he was waiting until of her own accord she gave him the response he was seeking. 'Touch me,' he murmured huskily. 'Kiss me the way you did when we were together in Wellington. Blot out these past six months as though they'd never been.'

But if she did, then what? Could she trust him, or would he later give her cause to regret bitterly the love she had given him in all its entirety? Surrendering all opportunity to ponder further, she pushed at him, rejecting him with a violence that was so unexpected, his response to it was spontaneous.

'Romy?' He too rose to his feet, concern and bewilderment in his face. 'What is it? What's wrong?'

'Nothing,' she mumbled, turning away. 'Nothing. I just feel like some fresh air, that's all.' She wrenched her raincoat off its hanger in the hall closet.

'But it's teeming down out there!'

'Go home, Quila,' she said, turning back to look at him. 'I want you to go home. I don't think things have changed between us after all. I don't think they can.' And pulling open the door, she started off down the flight of concrete steps, shrugging into her coat as she went.

Rain ran like cold liquid fingers through her hair, quickly plastering it to her scalp and saturating the upper regions of her coat until it lay in a sodden mantle across her shoulders.

Although eventually her steps slowed, she continued on in the rain, sheltered in brief snatches by the branches of evergreens overhanging the pavement. When there was no protection, she lifted her face mindlessly to the rain that descended like fierce tacks of ice over her skin, scouring it almost, and she wished its abrasive action had the power to reach every recess of her mind and heart and cleanse them just as easily of all her wretched thoughts, doubts and yearnings.

Perhaps it was the racket made by the rain watering the earth and plant life and washing the streets and the roofs and gutterings of houses, or simply her own preoccupation, which precluded her from hearing the rapid advance of footsteps behind her, and when her arm was taken in a grip which simultaneously apprehended and swung her around, she exclaimed aloud with fright.

'What the hell got into you, taking off like that?' Quila demanded, his glowering features partly revealed and shining wetly in the fluorescent rays of the nearby street light.

Recovering swiftly, Romy pulled her arm free. 'I told you to go home, and I meant it!'

This time Quila took her by both elbows and jerked her unceremoniously into his arms. 'The day that I begin heeding the orders of some demented, irrational female won't ever dawn,' he growled, 'so be warned. Now tell me what all this is about.'

Mutinously, Romy maintained silence and concentrated wholly on her struggle to be free of the manacles his hands made on her arms. 'Let me *go*!' she exploded at last.

'Tell me what I want to know,' he insisted with a grim calm.

'First let me go.'

'Not likely!'

She glared up at him and as a response he pulled her closer against him. 'Any more provocation,' he threatened, 'and I'll drag you off into the bushes, rain or no rain!' And his mouth descended to press briefly, savagely, not on but beside her own.

A clever stratagem, she thought as her fists clenched against his unbuttoned coat and her senses leapt in traitorous anticipation, only to cry out in mute disappointment when his lips failed to come into contact with hers.

Without haste, he caressed and explored with his lips each rain-washed feature while, in silence, she forced herself to maintain her stance of rigidity in his arms and hoped that her heart knocking so violently against her side wasn't transmitting its state of siege to him.

She thought she could succeed in holding out against him until the more persuasive moves of his teeth and tongue at her ear were her undoing. She made a token murmur of dissent, a feeble display of last-minute resistance, before surrendering herself totally, her body yielding, moulding itself to his, and her face turning, her mouth blindly even aggressively seeking his.

This time he neither denied her nor himself. A soft moan rose in her throat as he drew her so tightly against him, she was convinced that his arms would break her in two. When he broke the kiss long enough to murmur, 'At last,' Romy shook her head in protest. She didn't want conversation, no matter how brief, to be restored between them, not yet. She just wanted to prolong the feel and taste of his mouth on hers.

Explanations, self-recrimination and despair must be delayed for as long as possible. Thus, with her fingers splayed and threaded through his hair, she urged his head back down to hers, but he resisted as though suddenly sensing something was still amiss, and she felt the echo of deprivation in her heart.

'What is it, Romy?' he asked softly. 'What's troubling you?'

With her eyes still closed, she curled her fingers in his hair until strands of it were pulled tight. She must have hurt him, but he made no sound or effort to extricate himself. Instead, he lowered his head to the side of hers as, once more, she slowly sank back down on to the soles of her feet. She straightened her fingers and withdrew them from his hair. 'You're not staying,' she said flatly, her stare unwavering, and tried to draw away from him.

His arms slackened and she was permitted to step back but not to leave the circle of his arms altogether. 'I wasn't aware that I'd asked to.'

'No,' Romy granted him with faint cynicism. 'I suspect you were pretty sure that you wouldn't have to, that it would be *I* who would ask *you*. And then what would have happened, what ammunition would I have provided you with to fire back at me? What would you have accused me of?' She pulled sharply out of his arms and the barrier they had formed gave way immediately. 'This situation between us is no good. You may not want to compare me with your mother, but the fact remains you always will. Go back to Summerhaze, Quila. I don't want to see you again. I don't think . . .' Without warning, her voice broke. Blindly, she turned on her heel and began to half run and half walk back towards her flat.

'You don't think what?' Quila asked, catching up

with her just as easily as he had done the first time and grasping her arm in order to arrest her. 'Don't think what?' he insisted.

'I don't think I could bear it, that's what! Now leave me alone and—just go away!' She turned to jerk her arm free, but his fingers tightened their grip. 'You're hurting my arm!'

'Then for God's sake, Romy, stop running away from me! You've had your say. I listened. Now the least you can do is stay with me until you've heard what I have to say. All right?' he prompted when he failed to receive the affirmative response he sought.

Romy opened her mouth, but only to protest.

'All right?' Quila demanded, forestalling her.

Capitulating reluctantly, Romy gave a short nod of her head.

As they glared at each other beneath the stark white glow of the street lamp, she saw the purposefulness in his expression wane and one of uncertainty take its place. He had her attention and it seemed that he didn't quite know how to go about putting into words what was in his mind. 'I'm no Don Juan,' he told her simply, 'I never claimed to be and never wanted to be. I'm not saying that I've always lived like a monk, but . . .' he floundered a little in his search for the appropriate words with which to express himself. 'I guess I've always secretly hoped that one day I'd find someone special,' he confessed finally. 'I realise I haven't always treated you with the respect I should have, but one thing I've made myself learn in life and that is self-control. It'd be a pretty futile lie if I said I didn't want to make love to you, but the fact is, I wouldn't have stayed tonight even if you'd asked me to, and such an invitation wasn't what I was angling for. What I wanted above all was to win a response from you and try to guage from it whether or not you loved me—as much as I love you. I'm not sure of myself and never have been sure of myself with you, even in the beginning when I tried to hold myself aloof from you and convince myself that you couldn't possibly be as you seemed. And with Leon singing your praises morning, noon and night, it didn't help matters. Even so, I simply can't afford to let myself accept you don't love me.' He cupped her wet bemused face in his hands. 'Tell me that you do before I go insane!' And he kissed her gently until of her own volition she cast aside all reservations, repudiated all doubts, and went gladly into his arms.

Lifting his head at last, Quila seemed at first too overcome to speak, but contented himself with caressing her cheek with his and resting his forehead against hers. 'Passion,' he said huskily, 'between a man and a woman is a beautiful thing, but it was this response I was hoping for and will treasure above all. Do you believe me?' His eyes were earnest as they searched her face.

She nodded, capable of little else.

'You are precious to me,' he averred, 'and I want above all to love, honour and cherish you. Why don't you say something?'

'Because you're doing so well, I'm loath to interrupt.'

'Do I take it then that I can enquire about a marriage licence first thing in the morning?'

Romy relented then and laughed tremulously. 'Yes,' she answered, and with her joy overflowing, she slipped her arms up to hug his neck. 'Yes, a thousand times yes!'

HARLEQUIN
PREMIERE AUTHOR EDITIONS

6 top Harlequin authors — 6 of their best books!

1. JANET DAILEY Giant of Mesabi
2. CHARLOTTE LAMB Dark Master
3. ROBERTA LEIGH Heart of the Lion
4. ANNE MATHER Legacy of the Past
5. ANNE WEALE Stowaway
6. VIOLET WINSPEAR The Burning Sands

**Harlequin is proud to offer these 6 exciting romance novels by
6 of our most popular authors. In brand-new beautifully
designed covers, each Harlequin Premiere Author Edition
is a bestselling love story—a contemporary, compelling and
passionate read to remember!**

Available in September wherever paperback books are sold, *or* through
Harlequin Reader Service. Simply complete and mail the coupon below.

- -